Red Havoc Bad Cat

(Red Havoc Panthers, Book 3)

T. S. JOYCE

Red Havoc Rebel

ISBN-13: 978-1546344674
ISBN-10: 1546344675
Copyright © 2017, T. S. Joyce
First electronic publication: April 2017

T. S. Joyce
www.tsjoyce.com

All Rights Are Reserved. No part of this book may be used or reproduced in any manner whatsoever without written permission, except in the case of brief quotations embodied in critical articles and reviews. The unauthorized reproduction or distribution of this copyrighted work is illegal. No part of this book may be scanned, uploaded or distributed via the Internet or any other means, electronic or print, without the author's permission.

NOTE FROM THE AUTHOR:

This book is a work of fiction. The names, characters, places, and incidents are products of the writer's imagination or have been used fictitiously and are not to be construed as real. Any resemblance to persons, living or dead, actual events, locale or organizations is entirely coincidental. The author does not have any control over and does not assume any responsibility for third-party websites or their content.

Published in the United States of America

First digital publication: April 2017
First print publication: April 2017

Editing: Corinne DeMaagd
Cover Photography: Wander Aguiar

DEDICATION

This one's for the Heathens.

Questionable behavior.
Sassy mouths.
Loyal as hell.
My people.

ACKNOWLEDGMENTS

I couldn't write these books without some amazing people behind me. A huge thanks to Corinne DeMaagd, for helping me to polish my books, and for being an amazing and supportive friend. Looking back on our journey here, it makes me smile so big. You are an incredible teammate, C!

Thanks to Wander Aguiar and his amazing team for this shot for the cover.

To my cubs, who share me with the voices in my head. Thank you for being incredibly patient and always supportive and for bringing me surprise snacks on those big-work days.

And last but never least, thank you, awesome reader. You have done more for me and my stories than I can even explain on this teeny page. You found my books, and ran with them, and every share, review, and comment makes release days so incredibly special to me.

1010 is magic and so are you.

ONE

Barret Turgard narrowed his eyes at the quiet woods that surrounded the old tree house, then looked up into the branches of the ancient oak in front of him. "Lynn?" he called out, hoping to God she was in her human form. Her panther was just as psychotic as She-Devil.

The only answer was the soft rustle of fabric up in the little cabin someone had built into a tree long before Ben set up the Red Havoc Crew here. She wasn't answering. Typical female, makin' shit difficult.

With an irritated sigh, he placed the bag of groceries on his hip and made his way up the narrow staircase to the front deck of the house, up high in the canopy. It was covered in dead leaves and debris, and he kicked a couple of fallen branches out of the way of the door. The tree house was built between three white oaks that had grown in a triangle shape. A large porch surrounded the entire small one-bedroom tree house. The wood had gone gray with age, but it was holding together. And whenever a board rotted, he or Greyson just replaced it and kept the tree house viable. For reasons he couldn't explain, this place had always felt important to maintain. And now lookey here…Lynn had made it her own little Castle de Crazy.

Knocking was for the well-mannered, so Barret just barged in like he always did.

Lynn was sitting exactly where he knew she would be, in front of the back window, in an old neon-pink plastic lawn chair, staring at the tree branches outside.

He hated coming here, *hated* it. Hated seeing the girl he'd once known to be strong and capable like this, but it was necessary. He wasn't protective over much, but Lynn had been destroyed by what her last mate had done. Barret wished he could kill Brody all over again.

"I brought food," he said gruffly.

Lynn turned slowly in her chair. She'd always been a pretty woman, but now her cheeks were pale, her eyes hollow, and her smile empty. Her panther was tearing her apart from the inside out. Sometimes wrecked mating bonds did that. He'd watched this before, and Barret knew what was coming. Someday soon, Benson Saber, alpha of the Red Havoc Crew, would have to put Lynn down.

Barret busied himself with unloading the groceries into the small pantry and mini-fridge off the kitchen, but stopped when he thought he heard a whisper. Lynn hadn't talked much lately, so Barret frowned at the back of her head. "Did you say something?"

Lynn's voice came out scratchy from disuse. "My bird is back."

"You taking up bird watching now?" Huh. At least she was showing interest in something. "That's real nice, Lynn. I don't know jack-squat about no birds, but it's probably not as boring as watching curling, or turtle races, so that's cool." Maybe he could pick her up a bird guide in town on his way home from work tomorrow.

Light footsteps sounded on the stairs of the tree house, prickling his sensitive ears. Was it Greyson? He could've sworn it was his week to feed Crazy Lynn. But no, that wasn't right. Greyson might be a big cat shifter, but he was heavy-footed. Whoever was coming up those stairs was too quiet to be Greyson.

"Bird," Lynn murmured, staring out the window. Indeed, there were birds chirping and hopping on the branches outside. "I called to my bird and she came."

Footsteps were on the front deck now, crunching across the leaves. Who the fuck would be visiting Crazy Lynn besides him and Greyson? The fine hairs stood up all over his body. Something was wrong. A snarl blasted from his chest as he bunched his muscles defensively.

"You used to be fun, but you're different now," Lynn said without turning around. "I remember you in the beginning. At first, you hid your demons so well. You weren't so dark. Now they're scratching at you. Scratch, scratch, making you no fun."

The footsteps on the porch faltered and stopped.

"What do you mean?" Barret asked low. Lynn was creeping him the fuck out right now.

"You should be fun again." Lynn turned enough so he could see her profile. Her eyes were rimmed with moisture, and a single tear streaked down her cheek. "Never fall in love."

Barret looked around the tree house—really looked. There was a pallet on the ground by Lynn's bed and a second toothbrush on the sink. "Lynn, who's been staying here with you?"

It wasn't her mate, Brody, because that asshole was cold in a shallow grave somewhere. And to his knowledge, Lynn didn't have family close enough to lean on. She just had him and Greyson. They were the only ones she let up here. There had better not be some man up here taking advantage of her. He would rip his guts out and piss on the carcass.

"Who?" he repeated.

Lynn gave her attention back to the window. "The bird."

Chills blasted up his skin. Her words were foreboding, as if warning him of ghosts.

Lynn was bat-shit crazy, but right now, she couldn't protect herself. If it was a fucking Cold Mountain lion staying nights in the tree house, he was going to murder him right here on the front deck and leave him for the crows to eat. With a snarl, he strode for the door and yanked it open, ready to light into whoever was trying to take advantage of Lynn while she was down.

No one was there, though. The deck was empty except for leaves, branches, dirt, and a single brown and green tackle box. Feeling watched, he scanned the entire area, but he was alone out here. Slowly he bent at the knees and opened the tackle box, but what he found inside made no sense.

The little compartments were full of girl shit—eyelid glitter, face pencils, ten shades of pink lip slime, and in the bottom was at least twenty nail paints in different colors of the rainbow.

"Ew," he groused, letting the lid fall back into place. It created a breeze that lifted something soft and white into the air before it settled back on top of a pile of crisp, dead leaves.

Barret narrowed his eyes and pulled the small white feather in front of his face. No wild birds around here were this color. He'd seen this before—a snowy owl shifter, and that explained how Lynn's "bird" had escaped so quickly.

This fucker was messing with Lynn, and yeah,

Lynn was a nut-job, but she was also crew. And as much as Barret pretended to dislike Red Havoc, being crew meant something to him that he would never admit to the others because they would pity him. He fucking hated pity. Pity Kitty. Fuck that. He was tougher than all of them. He'd had to be to survive.

He stood and made his way to the railing and locked his arms on the splintered wood, scanned the branches for the trespasser. Whoever he was, he wasn't here. Coward.

In a monotone, Lynn repeated, "Never fall in love," through the open doorway.

Barret wanted to laugh. She wouldn't worry if she got a peek into his fucked-up head. All he could think about was the trespasser in Red Havoc territory and a dozen different ways to murder him.

He wasn't planning on falling in love.

He was planning a bird hunt.

****

Eden Brown closed her eyes tightly and hoped to God that scary-sounding man didn't see her. He'd growled so loud she could hear him plain as day through Lynn's door.

Right now, she could feel his gaze boring into the

tree she was hiding behind. Could he see the edges of her feathers? She pulled her wings in tighter and held her breath. Was he coming this way? Lynn could be scary quiet, so maybe he was too. It was the panther in Lynn that made her a good stalker. She'd always played sneak-attack on Eden when they were kids. That man had to be one of her crew. Greyson maybe? Or Barret?

Lynn didn't talk much anymore but had told her the only people she let into her tree house were the single panthers in the crew—Greyson and Barret. She hated the mated ones. Her panther would fight them. She didn't used to be like that. Before Brody, she'd been funny, light, and smiled all the time, and she was in control of her animal.

Brody had broken her, but Eden was determined to put her back together.

A limb snapped right under her tree, and terrified, she eased her eyes open. She expected to see the scary man staring up at her with gold eyes, the same color Lynn's got when she was about to Change or anytime Eden asked her about Brody or her baby daughter, Amberlynn.

The man was down there, but he was walking

past her tree. Eden's heart drummed against her breast bone, and her feathers ruffled up from the shock that zinged through her body. She watched in awe the tall man with the graceful strides make his way past her. His short hair was a chestnut color, but when he walked through the sunlight that speckled the forest floor, the light threw shades of copper throughout his hair. But it was his face as he strode by that held her attention. It was all sharp angles, a cleanly-shaven jaw, and a hard set to his mouth. He was the most striking man she'd ever laid eyes on, but from here, it looked like he had no smile lines at all. Pity. He lifted his nose to the air every few steps as if he was scenting it. Three steps, scent, three steps, scent. He wore a black T-shirt that hugged rippling muscles. His shoulders were as broad as a doorway, and his waist tapered to a sexy V-shape. His jeans hung low on his hips as though he didn't wear a belt, and his old work boots were all scuffs and dust. Something about him reminded her of home, but that made no sense. She'd never seen the man before. It was probably the work clothes. He would fit right in around Damon's Mountains.

In his hand was something small and white.

Eden's vision was impeccable in this form. He was holding one of her feathers, but why?

As he walked away, his chin lifted time and time again, as if he was checking the branches above him. Oh, that growly man had her ticket. He knew there was a flight shifter in these woods. Maybe she should just flit down to the forest floor, make a smooth Change, and introduce herself.

But just as she had almost convinced herself to greet him, he turned suddenly, showing his profile. His lip was snarled up in aggression, and his eyes were glowing a surprising green color instead of panther gold. They were almost as bright as Beaston's from the Gray Back Crew, and were just as terrifying, so she kept still, praying he wouldn't turn all the way around and see her.

Every instinct in her body screamed that the man walking away from her was dangerous, and she should let him leave. But that couldn't be right, could it? What little Lynn had said about Barret and Greyson, they sounded like they took care of her. Not emotionally, clearly, but they took care of her basic needs. A mean man wouldn't do that...right?

But then again, her instincts on men couldn't be

trusted. Her animal could be blamed for that. Eden's curiosity needed to stop here. She wasn't in Red Havoc territory to befriend the local hermit crew of panther shifters. Eden was here for Lynn, and Lynn alone. Her friend needed her, and if she was going to help, if she was going to keep Benson Saber from pushing Lynn out of his crew or worse, Eden needed complete focus on her. Not on some attractive man with a predator streak.

Greyson or Barret, she didn't care.

She just needed to get Lynn back on her feet and then get back to Damon's Mountains where it was safe for a shifter like her.

TWO

One head of lettuce, sixteen frozen burritos, seven cans of Ranch Style Beans, a dozen juice boxes, one loaf of bread, one jar of peanut butter, one spaghetti squash, and three tubes of toothpaste. That's what the scary cat had brought Lynn to live on for a few days.

No wonder she'd dropped weight.

With an irritated sigh, Eden pushed her shopping cart up the aisle faster. She needed to get back to the tree house, but Lynn needed healthy food in her diet. Her body needed to get stronger along with her mind. Tonight, Eden was making spaghetti and garlic bread and mixed vegetables. Tomorrow was steak. She needed to ease her friend back on lots of red meat to sate her inner panther. Peanut butter sandwiches and burritos didn't cut it.

She whipped the cart around the corner and crashed into another cart so hard the back wheels lifted off the ground by an inch and slammed back down onto the dingy tile.

"Oh!" she cried, startled beyond belief as she settled her gaze on the man from the woods. Her heart drummed against her sternum double-time as he narrowed his eyes and dragged his gaze down to her breasts, encased in one black, low-cut, V-neck cotton shirt.

He was staring, so she shifted her weight uncomfortably and then eased her cart slowly backward.

"Nice skull," he murmured, pointing to her boobs.

Oh. Right. She did have a white skull on this shirt. Maybe he wasn't a perv after all.

"Also nice tits."

Fantastic. Eden cleared her throat loudly and reversed into the aisle she came from. "Sorry," she murmured. "For, you know, running into your cart...bye-bye now."

But the man followed her, keeping their carts

nose-to-nose as she made her way backward down the cookie aisle. Without taking his eyes off her, the man reached out and scooped four packages of chocolate chip cookies into his cart, his clear green eyes daring her to say something.

Irritated now from being bullied down the aisle, she skidded to a stop and gave him her most ferocious frown—which was probably pathetic because she was completely intimidated by him. He was an entire foot and a half taller than her and nearly as wide as the damned aisle.

"I'm Barret, and I'm not made for a mate, so don't even fuckin' fall in love with me."

"Wh-what?"

"I see the way you're lookin' at me. Like you want my dick. Well, you can't have it. I don't bone humans." His eyes were too sharp on her, like he was gauging her reaction.

Poker face! "Soooo…you're one of those shifters?"

He had dipped his attention to her lips when she spoke. "Mmm hmm. Panther. You aren't a shifter groupie, are you?"

"Nope, not me. Well, it's been nice chatting with you." Kind of. He had complimented her shirt and tits, so there was that.

She made to turn her cart around, but he lurched forward and gripped the front, held it in place, and now he was too damn close. The air was thick, and it was hard to draw a deep breath with the pressure on her shoulders. Oh, he was a dominant brawler panther then, and she was in deep trouble if she didn't escape his calculating gaze soon.

"I told you my name. Now it's your turn."

"W-why do you want to know my name if you don't bone humans?"

"Because I like the way you look, and you smell like you would be a she-demon in the sack. You're all riled up just being around me. It's sexy. Name."

Eden's entire body had gone numb in the middle of his statement. She stood there like a tranquilized horse, staring at his perfect eyes, perfect cheekbones, perfect bad-boy smirk, perfect muscular throat, perfect line between his pecks as he said those filthy words. "I think you say things to shock people," she murmured softly. Well, at least the word combination made sense, so victory. She'd been afraid she would open her mouth and all that would come out was, "Ploof."

"You handled it well. You look a little flushed, though. I like it. I like that I get under your skin. You're an easy blusher. I bet if I smacked your ass in the bedroom, it would make a perfect pink handprint. Wouldn't it?"

"Ploof."

His devil-may-care smile stretched his face slowly. Lowering his voice, he said, "You ever had a man smack your ass, Mystery Girl? Some women don't like it, but I think you would the way I'd do it to you. I'd make it quick. Make it sting for just a second while I'm making you come. I would confuse your body. Pain and pleasure at the same time. I could make you come harder than you ever have before. Cookie?"

The last word caught her off-guard since she'd been so immersed in naughty-talk storytime.

Barret ripped into a package of chocolate chip cookies and offered her one. "Cookie?" he repeated, canting his head as if he hadn't just destroyed her ovaries with his words. She really wanted a spanking now. A spanking and a cookie. That was a first.

"You shouldn't do that," she reprimanded him, dropping her gaze to where his giant, meaty hand gripped the nose of her cart. "You haven't paid for it yet."

"But I will."

"It's against the rules."

"What rules? There aren't rules posted on how you can shop, Mystery Girl."

She huffed a frustrated breath. "Against basic moral rules. You're a rule breaker."

"Ooooh, you're a good girl then. A goody-goody. Straight As, perfect family, got into a good college, probably saved your V-card for just the right guy."

How dare he pretend to know her life? Anger churning in her veins, she said, "Wrong."

He called her out. "Lie."

"What about you?"

His lip snarled up into a feral expression that chilled her blood. "Guess, Mystery Girl. See how close you can get to figuring me out."

"Bad boy, bad cat, rule breaker, bad grades in school, cut class, didn't care enough about any one thing so you quit on everything you were decent at because you are a self-sabotager. You talk dirty to get a reaction out of people, but that doesn't fuel you like you wished it did. It makes you feel empty after you walk away. You break rules because you like to pretend you are above them. And you're snarling right now because I got closer than you thought I would. Let go of my cart."

The smirk long-gone from his face, Barret unhanded her cart and took a step back, chin lifted high, looking down his nose at her as his eyes blazed a brighter green. "Tell me your name. I want to know it."

"Because I called you out? Nobody does that to you, do they?"

"Wrong. Everyone calls me out, Mystery Girl. They just don't look sexy as fuck doing it. Name." The last word came out tapered into a snarl.

She dared a smirk like he'd given earlier. "My name's Mystery Girl. Enjoy your stolen cookies, Bad Cat."

Eden locked her gaze on his for a second more, then primly turned her cart and walked away. Yeah, she was wearing skin-tight jeans and swishing her hips a little more than necessary in them, but there was a hundred-percent chance that sexy man was watching her walk away. She felt like she'd just won some game he'd made the rules for, and yeah, she was feeling pretty proud of herself for not backing down in front of a pushy, brash, filthy-talking, dominant-as-hell, mother-freakin' panther shifter.

Female flight shifters were usually submissive by nature, but Kellen Brown, second of the Ashe Crew and big, badass, scarred-up grizzly shifter, was her father, and he'd done well to teach her how to posture with dominant males.

Thanks for that, Dad, she thought as she lifted her chin a little higher in the air and made her way to the pasta aisle.

She would have to tell Lynn how she bested a boy.

Lynn would love that.

****

She thought she was slick. Barret watched her shake that sexy ass of hers with every step until she disappeared around the corner. He knew the list of registered snowy owls. He'd memorized all the flight shifters. Maybe she was unregistered, but if she was a goody-goody rule-minder, she would've probably given her name to the public without any fight.

He recognized her scent and that floral shampoo she used. Her scent had lingered at the tree house, just faintly, and he'd memorized it. What the hell was Lynn doing hanging out with a flight shifter anyway? She was a panther. She should have more pride than that.

He should go after Mystery Girl. He should make her talk to him more. He hated that she had guessed so close to the truth, but at the same time, it had made his dick go hard to watch the mousey woman look him dead in the eyes and call him on his shit.

Long, platinum-blond hair, sky blue eyes, pale skin the color of the paper plates he ate off and, fuck no, he wasn't that poetic so it was the best description of her face he could muster. Her eyebrows were so blond they were barely visible, but they'd arched delicately with surprise when he'd spoken, trying to shock a reaction out of her. And her tits? Those were tens. Pushed up high with a red bra visible just above the V-neck. She wore black skinny jeans with rips on the thighs, exposing sexy strips of flesh. He wanted to poke his finger into the destroyed fabric and see if her skin was as soft as it looked. And then he wanted to scratch her a little bit. Just a little bit. Just enough to get her writhing at his touch. She wore dark eye make-up shit, hooker-red lipstick, and the skull on her shirt matched the four-skull ring she wore on her pointer finger. Tough girl in a submissive body. Interesting.

She wasn't too bright, though. Mystery Girl didn't know she was being hunted. It was almost too easy. Pity she wasn't a male like he'd expected to be sniffing around Lynn when she was this close to a heat cycle. He'd been prepared to murder a male, but he would have to go easy with Mystery Girl. His inner animal had very few morals, but critters with vaginas got a free pass. It was irritating having his anger cool so fast over a trespasser in Red Havoc territory. He blamed those Grade-A tits. God, they would fill his hands, and his hands were big. Looked soft as water balloons peeking out from her shirt. Red was now his favorite color on earth, not because of the Red Havoc Crew, but because of the way her bra had looked so sexy against her pale skin. He wanted to fuck those titties. Maybe bite her, too. Bite her? A purr rattled up his throat, and he swallowed it back down. *Shut up, Murder Kitty*. God, he was crazy.

When he bent just a little, he could see Mystery Girl through the shelves of cookies. She had her back to him and was humming. Humming? She had a pretty voice, and he took an involuntary step closer to the shelves that separated them just to hear her better. She was humming one of those Beck Brothers songs in a pretty alto, complete with pitch-perfect vibrato and everything.

Marney used to sing like that. Dad used to call her his songbird—

Stop it! Fuck. The memory of his step-mom the last day he saw her battered his mind, and he winced away from Mystery Girl.

Angry, he jerked the cart toward the checkout lines and refused to look back. Fuck her for bringing up things he'd buried long ago. *Pretty voice. Pretty voice. My songbird.*

Barret shook his head hard and started slamming the food on the conveyer belt.

Sleep my boy
For I am here
To ease your fear
All safe and warm and mine, my boy...

"Stop it," Barret snarled.
The cashier was a high school kid, maybe

eighteen, freckles and acne and a deep well of confusion pooling in his eyes. "Are you okay, sir?"

Sleep my boy
For I am near...

"No, no, no..." he murmured, panicking.

And when you wake...

Barret bolted. Fuck the groceries. He was going to Change if he didn't escape this place and flee from Marney's pretty voice in his head.

He'd done so good to stay dead inside, and numb, and what had Mystery Girl done? She'd leached his interest with her damn mysteries, and then she'd sang, just like Marney used to do. Same voice. Same tone.

The only way he ever felt better was defending territory. By protecting his people. And since Red Havoc was his crew, protecting those mountains and the people they housed gave him purpose. It gave him drive because, yeah, that girl had been right. He self-sabotaged on the regular, but he would be damned if he did that today. Not because of her. Not because of the soft voice in the back of his mind begging him to remember things that would kill his human side and bring on the panther. But because he was better. He was as good as he was gonna get, and he wasn't going back. No spiral into darkness. Not this time.

That snowy owl was conjuring a Hell named Barret Turgard.

If she dared to trespass in his territory again, he was going to set her fuckin' world on fire.

THREE

Gah, this hunt was too easy. It wasn't even satisfying since Barret had such an easy mark. This wasn't like when he'd hunted down the people who broke him. Mystery Girl was pitiful. It was like she had no instincts at all.

Barret made a pissed-off tick sound and lowered his shotgun. Yep, he was crazy enough to bring one of his guns, and nope, he didn't give a single shit what that said about him. He'd been planning to wait until she Changed and clip her in the wing, chase her from the territory and revel in the fact that it was going to take a long damn time for her to repair her wing-arm before she could fly again. That would teach her to fuck with panther territory. Instead, the pretty snowy owl shifter was marching up the stairs with two bags of groceries cradled to her chest without even scanning the woods, like she felt safe here.

She was the opposite of safe! He was murder! He was vengeance! He was Barret the Barbarian, and now she was pissing him off even more. Why? Because all he had to do was scare her into Changing and shoot her in the wing, but instead his stupid traitor eyeballs were trained on her ass as she climbed the stairs. God, it was perfect. Round and big and more than a handful, and his hands were big. He wanted to bite it. No. He wanted to bite one side and grab the other so hard it left a red mark that everyone could see. That's if she walked around pantless like he did on Naked Saturdays. Mmmmm, she would look good swishing around his cabin in nothing but one of those thongs. Hot pink. Push-up bra. Also hot pink. No. No bra, titties swaying when she walked, but thong, perfect. He hoped she had big nipples. Her skin had hardly any pigment, probably like her white feathers when she was Changed. Her nipples were probably light pink. Fuck, he had the biggest boner right now. Stupid Mystery Girl. He pulled his phone out of his back pocket and took a picture of her so he could stare at it later.

He was supposed to shoot her, not bone her.

Irritated, Barret sighed a snarl and removed the shells from his shotgun, then laid it on the ground. He wasn't even fucking hiding. If she had turned around at any point in her travels up to Lynn's tree house, she would've seen him clear as day.

Probably lived some cushy life where she was never in danger. Must be nice!

Oh good, now he was turned on and jealous at the same time, and he hated everything.

Maybe he could bang her like…one time and then shoot her.

His inner panther growled.

"Well, what?" he muttered out loud. "This hunt is for you, you stupid-dick-cretin. You're the one who requires blood all the fuckin' time." He crossed his arms over his chest. Time to compromise with the cat. "Sixty-nine and then shoot her."

Another snarl rattled up his throat.

"Fiiine. She blows me, or maybe gives me a hand job, and then I shoot her."

When pain blasted through his center with the next snarl, he doubled over the burning sensation in his stomach. It felt like he'd swallowed a bonfire. He groaned and rocked as if that would keep his shattering pieces together.

"Are you okay?" a soft voice asked.

Barret jerked his gaze to Mystery Girl, standing ten yards off, looking concerned and so fucking pretty he wanted to go back to negotiating sex before he clipped her wing. In the sunlight, her eyes weren't just blue like he'd thought in the store. They were a light bluish-gray color he'd never seen, and her blond hair had even lighter highlights in the sun.

"Stay back," he growled. Stay back? Why the fuck was he protecting her? If the panther got a hold of her, great. Boring hunt complete. But the thought of her snowy owl between his teeth made him retch unexpectedly. "Something's wrong with me," he croaked out.

The woman shifted her weight from side to side and scanned the sky. The sky? *No, darlin'. Keep them eyes on me. That's where the real danger is. I'm the danger.* Hesitating only a moment more, she padded over to him and knelt down in front of him.

Her gaze drifted to the shotgun on the ground, and her face froze in a mask of worry. "Why do you have that?"

"To shoot your wing, Trespasser."

Fury washed through her eyes, and then, like she'd done it a million times, the woman picked up his weapon, cracked it open, checked the load was removed, and then snapped it back together. She laid it back down in place, barrel carefully angled away from him. And then she took the two discarded shotgun shells and shoved them in her pocket. "If you would've shot me, you would've had the blue dragon here within the hour, burning your precious territory and eating your ashes.

"The blue dragon? Damon Daye?" he asked. Well, that was unexpected. He knew all the registered snowy owls in Damon's Mountains, and none were female except for one Rebecca 'Beck' Croy, mate to the Beast Boar and mother to Air Ryder.

"You knew at the store, didn't you?" she asked, squinting her pretty eyes in anger. "You knew who I was and you pretended not to."

The ache in his middle had gone away the closer she'd gotten to him, and now she was sitting on her folded-up legs right in front of him like she wasn't afraid of him at all. Her instincts were broken—that was for sure and for certain.

"You should leave."

"No. I'm here to help Lynn."

"Well, Lynn doesn't need your help. She has me and Greyson."

"Peanut butter sandwiches and frozen burritos won't mend her soul, Barret."

"Neither will girly make-up and nail polish!"

"We used to do girl's nights. I'm trying to bring back her old self."

"Well, her old self would've never hung out with a flight shifter."

"Wrong, panther. We were best friends." Ooooh, her voice was getting angry and her little eyes were getting even squintier.

And his boner was getting harder. She was sexy all riled up.

"You're a pest," he said, "and you don't belong here."

"Because I'm a flight shifter?"

"Because you're a stupid diaper-baby feather-face." Barret hissed, but swallowed the sound. "Shit. I can do better."

"Don't bother. Cussing me out won't get you what

you want." She stood and strode toward the tree house but rounded on him before she got to the stairs. "I was actually worried about you. I saw you out here doubled over, and I wanted to help, but you're a jerk! Lynn invited me. She called me. I left my life because she's important to me, and I'm staying. I'm not getting bullied out of here by a man-child who is mediocre at swearing and probably has too many peanut butter sandwiches and popsicles in his diet."

"Rude," he accused her.

She jammed her finger at him and retorted, "You're rude!"

He grinned. He couldn't help himself. She was so fucking cute, like a pissed-off little hedgehog.

"This isn't funny, you—you—"

"Say something scathing," he dared her. "Make it burn."

"Assface!"

Barret snorted. "Whose mediocre at swearing now?"

An animal screech wrenched from her throat before she spun and stomped up the stairs of the tree house.

Barret watched her ass sway until she disappeared onto the top landing, and then he grinned down at his boner. She was making him into a pervert. This was awesome.

"One blow job," he negotiated with his panther. When a purr rattled up his throat, the smile fell from his face. "And then I'll shoot her," he tested.

The purr morphed into a snarl. Aw, crap. That had never happened before. His inner cat was a murder-machine only sated for short periods of time if he bled his crew members or hunted constantly. He had never once turned down the opportunity to hurt something.

His Bad Cat, as Mystery Girl had called him, was paying way too much attention to this woman. He wasn't hunting her anymore, not the way he was supposed to. He needed to get her out of the territory as soon as humanly possible, not just for his own well-being…but also for hers.

Because no woman, no matter how much they irritated him, deserved the attention of a monster like him.

FOUR

A stiff breeze blew in through the open window of Eden's truck, and she looked up at the sky out of habit. No falcons. Relief. She didn't feel safe outside of Damon's Mountains because of Mom's warnings. Falcons had either allies and enemies, no in-between. She'd been safe under the protection of the Ashe Crew, and of Damon Daye, but out here in the Appalachian Mountains with no crew behind her, she was exposed. There was a reason she wasn't registered, and it had to do with a war between two sides of the falcon-shifter culture that had been waged a hundred years ago and was still being fought between the Welkin Raiders and the Crestfall Warriors. The councils on both sides that used to make decisions for the war had been killed off one by one over the past three years, including her grandfather. Only a few members of the Welkin Raider Council remained, and they were in hiding as far as she'd heard. Without leadership, chaos had blown through the falcon culture like a tsunami, and now the war had re-ignited worse than ever with only the warriors to make decisions. Eden needed to stay off the radar of the falcons.

If she was found with no protection, she could be taken into the Crestfall Warriors as a breeder because of her lineage, her mother's bloodline, and the color of her feathers, or she could be killed by the Welkin Raiders. Safety in numbers, and out here, where she was helping Lynn, Eden was alone.

She gripped the steering wheel and frowned out the front window at the sign above the mechanic's garage. *Turgard Repair.*

Why couldn't she get Barret out of her head? Okay, yes, he was sexy as hell and set her nethers on fire for reasons she didn't understand, but he wasn't particularly nice. And he cussed a lot. That, and two days ago she had caught him with a shotgun he'd brought to aim at her. So why was she here thinking of excuses to see him? "To help Lynn," she murmured out loud. Even she could hear the lie in her voice, but whatever.

The mechanic shop was an old, small, red-brick building with cracks up the side wall. Both of the garage doors were open. Inside were two cars, an SUV and one of those sporty, old trucks with the restored engine exposed. A familiar pair of legs in holey, grease-stained jeans and shit-stomper work boots was hanging out from under the belly of the truck. One of his legs was bent, the other straight, twitching with the movement of whatever Barret was doing under the truck. There was a strip of bare stomach exposed that said he wasn't wearing a shirt, and now her nethers were warming again. He had to have some kind of magic panther mojo that brought the girls to him or something. Like a man-siren, calling her to his sex appeal.

She should run away.

I want to see his nipples.

No! She wanted advice on Lynn. Yes. Advice. Nothing more. And then she would run away. Or fly.

Blowing out a sharp breath, she shoved the door of her black Ford F150 open and hopped out. The second she shut it, Barret slid out from under the truck, his eyes narrowed on her.

"No," he said so loud it echoed down the street.

"No, what? I haven't even asked you anything."

She came to a stop right in the middle of a treasure trove of greasy tools, which she didn't have a guess at, peppering the concrete. Barret was frozen, hunched over like he didn't know whether to slide back under or stand up. The position made his eight-pack abs extremely defined. A little perverted part of her wished she could straddle his hips and rest her hands on the twin grease marks across his chest. And then roll her hips against his and see if she could get a man like him riled up. She bet he was a large man everywhere.

What the ever-lovin' hell is wrong with me?

"Um, I came to you for advice."

"Okay, yes, you should leave Red Havoc territory. Advice given. I got work to do."

Irritating man. Eden clenched her fists at her sides and tried again. "Advice about Lynn."

Barret growled and slid all the way out from under the truck. He sat up and rested his elbows on his knees, clasped his hands and angled his face as he squinted against the sunlight. His pupils constricted in the light, making his eyes look even brighter and greener. "How do you know Lynn?"

When Eden kicked the nearest wrench lightly with the toe of her sneaker, it made a soft metal sound across the asphalt. She didn't like telling strangers anything personal about herself, but Barret's snarl had ceased and he looked genuinely curious. Plus, it was the first time he wasn't scowling at her, so it felt like progress. She pulled up a rolling creeper that looked like the one Barret was sitting on and sat down. With just a second of hesitation to find her courage, Eden scooted closer to him until their ankles were almost touching. It was a test, but he didn't flinch away. Another victory.

Barret dragged his eyes slowly over her body, pausing on her chest, then down between her legs, her knees, her ankles. With hungry eyes, he flickered his attention back to her face. "You don't have very good instincts, Bird Brain."

"My name is Eden."

His eyes tightened at the corners just slightly. "You aren't registered."

"Have you been researching me?"

"No. Stalking you. Again, your instincts suck big hairy balls."

"Well, I've been stalking you, too. I found your shop, didn't I? Maybe you should be the one who's scared."

Barret snorted. "Of a flight shifter?"

"Maybe I'm not afraid of you because I grew up with monsters way bigger and meaner than you," she said primly.

"Like Lynn?"

"Lynn and I grew up together, yes. She was adopted when she was four by a couple that lives right outside of Damon's Mountains."

"Bullshit. Lynn's a panther, through and through."

"Yeah she is, but she was raised by tiger shifters. They kept her unregistered. Our parents kept as many of the kids unregistered as they could get away with."

"Why?"

"Safety. Probably the same reason you aren't registered."

"You don't know me," Barret muttered, shaking his head and staring out across the parking lot of his shop.

"Enlighten me then."

"No panther shifters register unless we're forced. There isn't that many of us anymore."

"Anymore?"

Barret gave her an empty smile. "Other shifters killed us off." He jerked, like he had a tick, but after he settled, he gritted out, "Fuck talking about this. What do you want?"

"How do I help Lynn?"

"Easy. You don't. She's screwed. I can see her panther eating her up from the inside out. I've fought that battle before."

"But you're still here. You won."

Barret huffed an angry breath. "I won part of the battle. Somebody should've put me down. It'll be better for Lynn if Ben takes care of her."

"Takes care of her? You mean if he kills her?"

"Yep."

"Do you have no concern for your crew member at all?" she asked, her eyes prickling at the thought of a world with no Lynn.

"You have it wrong. I care about her a lot. Fuck." He twitched again. "Don't tell anyone that." Barret snatched a dirty rag off the floor and stood, then paced away from her and back, wiping his hands on the stained fabric. "My crew. *My crew.*" He jammed a finger at her. "Lynn's mine, and so are the others, and I care enough to want her to escape what's happening to her. You ever seen a broken mate bond, Eden? Huh? I have. My dad went through it. My mom was human and left me and my dad in a crew full of mated panther pairs. My dad's bond was the only one that failed, and you know what he did?"

Horrified, Eden whispered, "What?"

"Nothing. He withered. He stopped working, he stopped eating, he stopped drinking. He…fuck." *Twitch.* Barret grabbed his hair and gritted his teeth as though in pain. He choked on the next admission, as if the words clogged his throat. "He stopped laughing, stopped hugging me, stopped tucking me in, stopped looking at me. He stared out the fucking window and got quiet for two years before Marney came along."

"Who is Marney?"

"Can't talk anymore." *Twitch.*

"Barret—"

"No!" He picked up a greasy carburetor and threw it against the wall so hard it got stuck in the sheetrock. Barret threw up his middle finger at the carburetor, just hovering in the wall, and then he strode through a side door next to it.

Eden sat there frozen, unsure what to do. His mood had changed so fast she should be terrified right now. The air had grown instantly heavier, clogging her lungs, and even though he was out of sight, the pressure of his dominance remained.

She should've left, but her inner animal screeched in rebellion at the thought.

Barret needed a friend. He needed someone to make him steady again.

Determined, she stood and kicked his discarded creeper out of the way, then made her way through the door where he'd disappeared. Inside, there was a checkout counter, a small waiting area, and a hallway. She was met with complete silence, but she could feel him. With each step she took toward the hallway, the air became thicker until it was like trying to breathe water.

The office door creaked as she pushed it open with her fingertips, and there he was. Barret wasn't pacing like a caged animal as she'd imagined he would be. He was crouched in the corner with his back to her, hands linked behind his head, shaking, resting the crown of his head on the wall. From this angle, she could see his only tattoo. It encased one shoulder and was so dark she had to squint to make out what it was. The artwork was some type of bird with its wings stretched. The flight feathers curved around his collar bone on one side and around to his shoulder blade on his back. The tattoo artist had been very skilled.

A constant snarl sounded from his throat, but the second she rested her palm lightly onto the back of his neck, the noise ceased. She thought he would flinch away and hole into himself, the way dominant males tended to do when they were cornered or hurt, but he shocked her to her bones when he reached up and rested his palm on her knuckles, keeping her hand in place on his skin.

"I like touch," he croaked out.

"Because of your panther?"

"I don't know."

"Because of your human side?"

"I don't know."

He was done giving her answers, apparently, so she knelt behind him and rested her cheek against his back, relaxed against him completely until he eased onto his butt and leaned into her. Slowly, she sat too, slid her arms around his middle, and encased his hips with her knees. And then she held him. She hugged him. She embraced this stranger in a moment that was becoming the most intimate she'd ever experienced. Eden didn't know how long they sat like that, but eventually, he sighed and relaxed against her completely. She brushed his skin, right over his abs, and a soft purr rattled up his throat. He didn't cut off the sound but let it happen. Behind his back, she smiled. Barret might be a tough guy, but he liked being petted.

She closed her eyes and inhaled slowly, committing his scent to memory. Oil, cologne, fur, and a hint of sweat that made her hormones do backflips.

"I'm sorry for what happened," she whispered.

"I didn't tell you what happened."

The smile dipped from her face. "What do you mean?"

"That wasn't the bad part," he rumbled "No more. Talking doesn't help. Not ever. Talking lets out my demons."

"Maybe they shouldn't be in cages. Maybe you

should just keep them on leashes."

He turned in her arms and settled his back against the wall. She thought he was shutting her out, but he grabbed behind her knees and dragged her whole body forward until they were almost connected at the hips, her legs bent over his, her ankles on either side of his waist. She loved this. It was as if she'd known him in no time at all and forever all at once. It made her dizzy and excited and scared and happy. Inside of her, the falcon was watching him quietly, possessively, as if he was already hers.

"You speak of demons like you have them, too," he murmured in a deep, raspy voice.

"Not me. I got lucky, but I was raised with shifters who were full of monsters. Damage is what I know."

"Things went wrong when I was young," he murmured. He flipped her palm over and stroked a finger along her life-line. "And when I think about how things went wrong, I panic and try to escape the bad stuff."

"By acting out?"

Barret shrugged up one shoulder. "If I don't get rid of the memories, the panther takes me."

"For how long?"

"Longest was three months."

"Oh, my gosh," she whispered. "Three months? I can't even imagine how much your body must've hurt when you Changed back to your human form."

Barret's lips twitched into a blank smile. "You think I don't care about Lynn, but I've seen her panther take her when she was trying to avoid thinking about Brody and Amberlynn. And it'll get worse. Sometimes it's best to put an animal down if it's suffering enough."

"I won't let it get worse for her."

"You won't have a choice." He looked up, and his eyes were a thousand years old. "Lynn's full of demons now too, and she isn't strong enough to lock them away."

Her heart felt like it was breaking inside of her chest cavity, as if being seared in two. She'd known Lynn was bad off, but she hadn't realized it might be too late to save her.

"Help me then. Help me help her. Help me *save* her."

He huffed a small laugh. "I'm Murder Kitty, not Rescue Kitty." He studied her face for a few moments before he said in a low voice, "You don't quit on people, do you?"

"Not ever," she answered truthfully.

Barret cocked his head and studied her, licked his lips and then pursed them in thought. "Spending so much time away from her crew isn't doing her any favors."

"Oh, I tried to get her to visit Red Havoc. She freaked out and Changed and nearly clawed my face off."

Barret's eyebrows jacked up in a challenge. "I gave you the advice you came for. I didn't say it was going to be easy, or even doable. You want a shot at saving her? Give her something to fight for again. Give her the crew."

"Is that what you did to save yourself?"

His smile turned wicked. "I. Don't. Know."

Walls. Barret was all walls. He was cinder block barriers that kept him separate from the outside world. Maybe it was a defense mechanism to protect his heart from further hurt, or perhaps his panther was so broken he required distance to stay steady. But here he sat, rubbing her palm, his legs relaxed under hers, gaze steady on her eyes, not running from her. He just refused to let her past the wall that shielded his soul from the world.

Barret was dangerous because he could pretend he didn't care, and it was believable. She'd assumed he didn't have any sympathy for Lynn, when the truth was he cared so much it cut him on the insides, more than he would admit.

Barret was a complicated mess. But for reasons she didn't understand, he felt like her complicated mess—one she wanted to unravel slowly until he would let her shoulder the burdens of his past with him.

He didn't trust her yet, but suddenly, she wanted to be the person who stuck around long enough to earn it.

Eden wanted to *earn* his story.

She arched her attention to his tattoo, to the wings, but he covered it with his giant hand and shook his head slowly. Wall.

Disappointment swirled in her chest. He was the type of man she would take one step forward with, but two steps back. That was his kind of dance. A sensible woman shouldn't want to keep pace with a man like him, but she already felt connected in some strange way. She should get up and walk out, leave him alone to his demons, forget him, focus on Lynn, go back to Damon's Mountains, be safe.

Safe. That had been her entire life since Mom had beat it into her head to keep her eyes on the skies and stay out of the talons of the Welkin Raiders. She'd lived her entire life for safety, dated only safe men, made safe friends, worked a safe job crunching numbers for Damon Daye in his mountains where the falcons wouldn't dare to come because they would risk the blue dragon burning them to nothing and devouring their ashes. And here she was, out in the open, exposed, in the territory of panthers, her attention utterly taken by the most dangerous kind of man to fall for—a dominant, broken one.

"You want to run," Barret accused her. "You've got one foot out the door already. Not surprising. I'm not made for a mate, not made for a woman, can't make one happy." He gave her a wild-eyed, feral smile. "Run, little bird. Don't let the big bad cat get you." Wall.

"Don't do that."

Barret rested his head back against the wall and looked down his nose at her. He was still covering his tattoo, his fingers digging into his skin, his abs flexing with each slow breath, his eyes blazing too bright a green to be human.

Before she could chicken out, Eden climbed onto his lap, straddled him until their pelvises touched. She rested her hands on either side of his neck and searched his eyes for a moment of hesitation before she leaned in and pressed her lips to his.

He jerked at the kiss, his lips stiff under hers for the span of three breaths before he grabbed the back of her hair and pushed his tongue into her mouth. Oh, he wasn't going to let her keep the kiss sweet. Wall.

When she rocked against his erection, he moaned softly into her mouth. Warmth unfurled in her middle. She rolled against him again, and he hit her just right, even through her jeans. God, this felt so good. She could come just like this.

Eden wanted to feel him, just one tiny touch. She brushed her fingertips into the waist of his jeans and felt the swollen head of his shaft. A drop of moisture at the tip clung to her fingers, and she smiled against his rough kiss. Sexy, sexy man. Now he was the one rocking his hips, chasing her touch, so she popped his button and slid her hand inside his pants, gripped his dick, and rubbed him to the hilt, slowly.

"Fuuuuck," he moaned.

She stroked him again, and he gasped and gripped her hair tighter when she got down low enough.

"I wanna fuck your mouth," he gritted out, guiding her head down. Wall.

Eden yanked back and dug her nails into his forearm. "No. I'm not sucking you off the first time we're intimate. We come at the same time or not at all."

His eyes flashed with intensity, and then before she knew it, she was on her back on the floor and Barret was ripping her jeans down her thighs. He shoved her shirt up over her head and unsnapped the front clasp of her bra like he'd taken damn lessons. His hand dug into her hip as he leaned forward and drew her taut nipple into his mouth, sucked hard enough to get a groan out of her. She gripped his hair to keep him there. Now this was more like it. Or at least she thought until he started kissing his way down her stomach to her panty line.

Wait. She'd made a rule. Right? Some sort of rule about them coming at the same time, for some sort of reason. Oh, God, he was pulling her panties down now and ohhhh, there was his tongue. He pushed her legs farther apart and plunged his tongue into her deeper and, holy hell, she was already close. The pleasure was so intense she would've done anything to make him keep going. Gripping his hair, she dragged him closer and rolled her hips against his mouth, arched her back against the floor and cried out.

His purr rattled against her sensitive sex as he gripped her hips hard, dragging her against his face every time he pushed into her with his tongue.

"I'm coming, I'm coming!" she yelled. He groaned against her, pushed in faster, and she shattered around him like glass. Orgasm blasted through her body, pulsing around his tongue as he licked her. He kept at it until she was too sensitive and twitching, until every last aftershock had been drawn from her body. Until she whispered his name and closed her eyes, relaxed against the floor.

Wait… In the haze of satisfaction, something pulled at the edges of her blown mind. "We were supposed to go at the same time."

Barret bit the inside of her tender thigh, almost

hard enough to break the skin and claim her, but he released her instead. "Best you don't make rules for a monster like me, little bird. Makes me want to break 'em." He got on his hands and knees and straddled her hips, then took himself in hand and began stroking his dick.

Eden was mesmerized, or shocked perhaps. She'd never seen a man do this, and he was owning it, eyes on her as he pushed into his hand faster and faster, harder until his hips bucked and he gritted out her name. She was so worked up, so excited, desperate for him to finish. *Please don't stop.*

He pushed into his hand again and froze as warmth spilled onto her belly. Another stroke, more warmth, and more and more until it was running down the sides of her ribs. His teeth were clenched, his eyes intense as he finished on her. He hadn't bitten her thigh, but in a way, this felt like a claim. It wasn't sex, but it was something big.

She thought he would stand up and walk out, throw up another wall, but instead he frowned and murmured, "I don't think I should've done that."

"Why?" she whispered.

He lifted her palm to his chest, right over his

heart, but she couldn't tell if he was trying to share how fast it was beating or the rattle of the purr that was working its way up through his torso.

Barret leaned down and plucked gently at her lips. He angled his face and brushed his tongue against hers softly as though coveting her. As though he was adoring her. He brushed his knuckles down her cheek, cupped the back of her neck, and kissed on and on.

And when at last he rested his forehead against hers and closed his eyes, seemingly content to just be like this, touching her, she realized something huge.

She was pretty sure he was a man who didn't allow it often, but Barret had just let her past the wall.

FIVE

Lynn's Change today had been bad. The panther had been aggressive and gone after Eden as if she didn't recognize her. At the last second, she'd had to Change and fly out of the panther's way. Lynn had shredded the clothes she'd left behind, even pissed on them for good measure, like she was mad at Eden for trying to help. It was as if the panther wanted the human part of Lynn to stay broken so the animal could have the body when she wanted. There was too big a disconnect between Lynn and her animal.

She had a plan, though. Or more specifically, Barret had come through and come up with a plan.

When Eden's phone chirped on the bathroom counter, excitement flooded her chest. Barret had asked for her number, and he'd done it sweetly. He'd knocked on her window right as she was about to pull away from his mechanic shop earlier. He'd struggled for words for a moment, shuffled his feet, and then blurted out, "I'll help with Lynn. We'll try to save her. Hope for the best and prepare for the worst and all. I need your number. No." He'd shaken his head and scratched the back of his hair in an irritated gesture. "Can I please have your number? To call you. Or text you?"

He inhaled and let off a quick breath, then opened his mouth to dig himself in deeper, but she'd interrupted. "Yes. I'd like for you to call me. I mean, don't call me. That's a rule." Because reverse psychology.

The devil had been in his smile as she recited her number for him to save into his phone.

When she'd arrived at the tree house, Lynn had been writhing on the forest floor, fighting a Change, and Eden had been wracked with guilt at taking so long. Now she was washing Lynn's hair in the bathtub so she could soak her sore muscles in some Epsom salts. Lynn Changed too much. Too many shifts were hard on the body. She never complained, but even now, Eden could see her muscles twitching with discomfort. Her friend had always been tough.

She looked at her phone and smiled at Barret's short message. *Almost ready. Good luck. p.s. you taste really fucking good.*

The last part made her cheeks heat with pleasure. She didn't know why that was so flattering. Barret was wild, and likely more animal than man, but he'd just put to rest any insecurities she could've had about him going down on her. Good man.

"Why are you smiling like that?" Lynn asked from where she was sitting tits-deep in bathtub water. She didn't talk much so her voice had come out hoarse. Her red hair was soaking and plastered to her flushed cheeks, and her soft brown eyes were narrowed with suspicion. "Who texted you?"

"Barret."

Looking panicked, Lynn gripped the edge of the bathtub. "Why does he have your number?"

"Because he invited us to dinner with Red Havoc. He's barbecuing ribs."

"Oh." Lynn relaxed by a fraction and sank back away from the edge. "Ribs used to be my favorite."

"Used to be? What's your favorite now?" Lynn

hadn't talked this much in a long time, not coherently, so Eden was going to drag this conversation out as much as possible.

Lynn blinked slowly, and her eyes glazed over. "Nothing is my favorite anymore. I don't like the boys. I want food but not with the boys. I would rather starve."

"There're females in the crew now. Two new ones. Annalise and Kaylee. One is a panther shifter and one is a brand-new lioness. Barret says they're both nice when they're human."

"Girls," Lynn repeated absently, playing with a long strand of wet, copper-colored hair. "I don't like the boys. I want you to go get the ribs. You go eat with the boys. Don't fall in love. Bring me food back. I want to be alone with my bird."

Eden frowned. "*I* am your bird, and I want you to come with me. I don't want to meet your crew alone. You should be there."

"Can't." Lynn shook her head slowly. "Just can't."

Fuck. A little wrinkle of stubbornness formed on the bridge of Lynn's nose that said she wouldn't be moved on this.

"It's okay, I'll just stay here. With you."

"I want you to go away. Go to Red Havoc." Lynn's eyes were churning with a fury Eden didn't understand. "I want to be alone. I'm never alone."

Eden narrowed her eyes. "You've been alone too long. I think that's the problem and remember, Lynn, you were the one who called me here. The only reason I'm here is for you, not to rub elbows with your crew."

"Not crew. Barret. Don't. Fall. In. Love." Lynn got out of the bathtub, splashing and dripping everywhere, and strode directly out of the bathroom, dove into her bed, then pulled the blanket over her head. "Seriously, Eden. I need time alone."

Eden stared at the unmoving lump in the bed for a long time, but Lynn was snarling. If she got angrier, she would Change again, and it would hurt her. Finally, Eden murmured, "I'll be back in an hour."

The growling stopped. Shaking her head at how wrong this felt, Eden made her way to the door and grabbed her wallet. She didn't carry a purse, but since their plan had failed, she had full intention of paying Barret back for the groceries he'd bought.

Already, she knew the Red Havoc woods like the back of her hand because she'd flown them several times since she'd been here. Her animal missed nothing. The cabins were within walking distance, and it was a nice evening, so she pulled on a pair of hiking boots over her skinny jeans and made her way out of the tree house to the forest floor. A confusing mixture of guilt over leaving Lynn and excitement over seeing Barret swirled in her chest, making her feel light-headed.

The woods here were so different from Damon's Mountains in Wyoming. Even the bird sounds and the tenor of the creaking trees were different. Sunlight filtered through the canopy, speckling the ground in yellows and golds, and all around was the music of life, from the rustling leaves in the wind to the tiny field mice moving carefully through the leaves around their tiny homes. She checked the sky, but there were no giant falcons coming to kill her or kidnap her away for some barbaric breeder program. The falcons only valued females for genetics, and her feathers were white. Damon Daye said she was the only albino falcon shifter, and she would be coveted in the falcon's breeding program if they ever found out about her. With a relieved puff of breath she expelled from her lungs, she dragged her attention back to the woods, and suddenly she wasn't alone like she'd thought.

Barret stood leaned against a tree, still as a stone, his green eyes narrowed calculatingly on her, his arms crossed over his chest, making his biceps look even bigger somehow.

"Something is wrong," he said so softly she almost missed it.

"Yeah, Lynn won't come."

"No...I mean with me."

Eden slowed and stopped five yards in front of him. He felt too heavy, too dominant, too riled up, but his eyes were clear and forest green instead of his panther's blazing moss green.

"Are you okay?" she murmured.

He shook his head slowly. "I've never been okay. And now my head is all filled up with you." Something about the way he said that reminded her of the way her dad spoke to her mom. But Barret was big and strong and capable. He hadn't been broken like her father had...had he? Kellen, her dad, had been brought up by a cruel father until he found a home with Tagan, the alpha of the Ashe Crew, when he was ten. Because of his broken animal, Eden had been brought up to recognize damage in others, especially in shifters. She was familiar with it…sensitive to it.

Barret scrubbed his hand down the short stubble on his jaw, and when she took a step toward him, he backed up one to match, keeping the distance between them intact. It hurt like a slap and made her angry she could feel pain like that from a man this soon.

"I haven't been single for long," she said.

A growl rattled his throat, and he took another step back. "Don't tell me."

"No, you should hear why your moving away hurts. I watched all my friends grow up and find mates and move out of Damon's Mountains. One by one, they left, and I was stuck. I didn't attach to men, I don't know why. I didn't find my mate, and each year, I grew lonelier and sadder and emptier because my inner animal wanted companionship. She craved it. I met Marcus, and I thought he hung the moon. I thought I was out of my slump and normal after all, like my friends who had found their other halves. But he didn't like touch. He didn't like *my* touch. I felt repulsive and plain and invisible and unimportant for an entire year before I left."

"Why did you stay with him that long?"

"Because I thought no one else would want me. Because I was scared of starting over and not finding my person. Because I'm loyal, and my heart latches onto things that hurt me, and I have trouble letting go."

Barret gave her a cruel smile. "You're doing it again. Don't get loyal on me. I hurt everyone, and you'll be no different. Stop fucking with my head, Mystery Girl."

"You're being mean."

Stooping, Barret picked up a small rock and then moved toward her. He held out the flat of his palm, and on it sat the offered rock.

"What's this for?"

"To remind you."

"Of what?"

"That I can't stay nice for long."

Fury blasted through her veins. It was such bullshit. It was a copout. It was him throwing up another wall after he'd let her see through the cracks and into his soul earlier. She took the rock and chucked it as hard as she could into the woods. And then before she could change her mind, she threw her arms around him and hugged him. No…hugging would be intimate. She squeezed his arms, pinning them to his sides as hard as she could. She wasn't hugging him. She was trapping him against her as punishment.

He struggled. "Stop it."

"You stop it. You gave me a good moment earlier. You made plans with me to help Lynn, and you're doing it."

"I don't know what you're talking about." Barret struggled harder and hissed long and low as he backed into a tree. "Stop!"

"You're trying to make me feel alone again."

Barret went still and stared off into the woods with dead eyes, his back against the rough bark, every muscle in his torso tense against her. A stone statue would've been softer to embrace than him.

It felt like hours before he swallowed audibly and rasped out, "You don't know what being alone is like. You grew up in Damon's Mountains, safe and protected. I'm the one who will always be alone. Best you don't talk about shit you know nothin' about."

"You're wrong. I know loneliness. I'm rare. I'm unregistered. Yeah, I was in Damon's Mountains, imprisoned all my life so I could survive. I was part of a crew, but the only kid like me. On the inside and the outside all at once."

"My crew is dead." His voice came out flat and emotionless.

Baffled, she eased back and loosened her grip on him. "W-what? No they aren't. Red Havoc is okay. I've seen them."

"Red Havoc wasn't supposed to be my crew. I had a family, friends, other panthers just like me. Red Havoc is the replacement so I can hold onto my skin longer."

"What crew?"

He shook his head for a long time, denying her an answer, but she wasn't going to bend on this one. She had to know what had happened that made Barret so closed off. What had happened that an entire crew had died. Fire? Poison?

"My crew was the Four Deadlies."

A sharp gasp inflated her chest. Eden was so shocked she released him in a rush. No. No, no, no, that couldn't be possible because all the panthers in that crew had been killed off by falcons. By their war. "The Four Deadlies?" she repeated, hoping to God she'd heard him wrong.

Barret's eyes narrowed into suspicious little slits. "Do you know what happened to them?"

Murder. It wasn't poison or fire or a bus accident. They'd been murdered for harboring a female falcon shifter. The Four Deadlies had gotten in the middle of the falcon wars, and the Crestfall Warriors had exacted a horrific revenge. To get to the runaway falcon, they'd wiped out the crew. Barret's crew.

"How old were you?" Damn her voice as it shook.

"Ten."

Just like Dad had been when he'd had to make a new life. No wonder Barret was so devoted to building his walls. "Do you...do you remember?"

"It ain't exactly something a boy forgets." Barret's face ticked into a feral expression before it settled back into a hard, stoic mask. "Smell that, bird? Meat. Dinner's on." And with that, Barret gave her one last fiery glance and walked away. He made it exactly four steps before he yelled, "Shit," loud enough to echo through the woods. He spun on his heel and strode toward her, his eyes burning like green flames. He crushed her to his chest so fast and so hard it stole her breath away. "You aren't alone. You're in my head, filling it up until I can't think of anything else. Even when you go, a stupid piece of me will be with you. Stupid because I know what's happening here. I can see it coming. You're a firecracker with too much powder. You're a tornado, and you're sweeping me up so you can toss me somewhere I don't recognize. And when you fix Lynn or get her killed, you'll go back to your safe life, and I'll be here, feeling even worse than I did before." He heaved a frustrated sigh that tapered into a growl. "And I like the way you hug me like a psychopath!" He released her and steadied her, hands on her shoulders, until she stopped swaying on numb legs, and then he leaned down and kissed her hard. There were no soft lips or sweet smacking sounds.

Barret was wrong.

He was the tornado, and he'd pulled her into his intensity from the second she laid eyes on him. And now he would be the one tossing her somewhere she didn't recognize, and already, *already*, and horrifyingly, her heart was changing.

Any man who could do that—change a heart—was the most dangerous type of man to fall for. He had too much power, and she was falling straight into him. Straight into the chaos of Storm Barret.

And she wasn't scared like she should be! She wasn't proceeding with caution like a wise woman. Instead, she had this overwhelming urge to collect his *stupid* pieces until she had them all.

Selfishly, she wanted to keep him. Not out of a sense of guilt over falcon shifters taking his crew from him, no. She was in this because of this right here—his lips on hers, demanding she let go. Demanding she close her eyes and let the storm sweep her away.

Don't fall in love.

Lynn's voice was just a whisper in her mind, as quiet as a breath and easily ignored. Barret wasn't running now. He wasn't afraid of her touch or throwing up his defenses. He was letting go just like she was. Eden smiled against his lips in triumph as he slowly softened the kiss. Now he was all fingertips tracing her jaw, pushing her hair back off her shoulders, brushing her neck, gripping, gripping, a soft brush of tongue and then the sweet sipping. She never wanted it to stop. He wasn't pushing for more, but he wasn't easing them out of the kiss either. He was just enjoying her, like she was him.

And then at last, minutes or perhaps hours later, he kissed her one last time and took a step back, looking as baffled as she felt. Eden bent down, picked up a rock from the ground, and then offered it to him, palm up.

"What's this for?" he asked low.

"It's to remind you that you can be nice to me."

Barret's eyes flickered from the small brown stone in her hand to her eyes and held her gaze. She would've given everything she owned to know what he was thinking in this moment, but the coward inside of her was too afraid to ask. Without a word, he plucked the rock lightly from her palm, brushing the skin there so gently as he did, then put her gift into his pocket.

She wouldn't tell him but, by accepting her rock, he'd just bound her to him in ways he would never understand. Falcons exchanged gifts. She'd never offered anything to a man, had never had the urge to, but the need to give him this tiny gift had consumed her, had made her feel reckless just to see if he would reject it. Barret would probably throw it away the second she wasn't looking, and that was okay. She didn't want to see him do it though, so she could pretend he kept it.

Don't fall in love.

She was a falcon, and falcons gave gifts when they chose their person.

It wasn't L-O-V-E yet, but she'd just arrived at the first letter.

SIX

Did Eden understand what she had just done?

Barret's fingers itched to touch the small stone that pushed against his denim pocket just to make double sure it was safe and secure. She'd thrown his rock into the forest when he'd tried to sabotage them, and then she'd rewarded his affection by giving him one with a more hopeful meaning instead. She'd basically told him she believed in him. She did! What else could it mean that she would point out that he was capable of being nice?

And now they were here, walking side-by-side through the Red Havoc Woods like a normal couple getting to know each other. This was a moment he'd never in a million years thought would belong to him.

"I didn't get presents for a long time," he admitted. God, it was so hard to say those words. "When my crew...well, after they were gone, I was on my own a lot." He cast Eden a sideways glance to gauge her reaction. His upbringing hadn't been a normal one like hers. He needed to figure out when he was being too much so he could dial it back and trick her into staying longer. Her lips were downturned and her eyes full of sadness, but she wasn't running yet. So he shared more, just to test her a little bit. "One day I was acting out. We were eating at this burrito place, and Kaylee brought her cub to meet the crew for the first time. Bentley. That's her son's name. Anyway, he reminded me of me when I was a cub because he didn't have a pride or a crew for a long time. It started scratching at all these stupid memories I have to keep tucked away, and I was trying not to give in and Change, so I was complaining about being hungry. I was mad that Kaylee had a cub, mad that Bently would be a part of us, mad that she was building a family with Anson, when I have no shot at having a family ever. But that kid...he listened to me panic about food, and he gave me a bean."

"A bean?" she asked, her moue turning into a slight smile. God, she was stunning, hair all wild, eyes trained on him, unafraid of the monster that sat just beneath his surface.

Barret chuckled. "Yeah, a single black bean. He was trying to share, but all I could do was sit there and stare. It hit me that it was the first present I'd gotten since I was a kid when my dad gave me a shotgun for my tenth birthday."

"What did you do with it?"

"The shotgun? Shot up every glass bottle and tin can I could get my hands on from age ten until now."

Eden giggled this pretty, tinkling laugh. "No, I mean what did you do with the bean?"

"Well, I tried to eat it, but Anson was a mega-dick and slapped me in the head and made me spit it out."

Her giggle bubbled from her chest, and he reveled in the sound. He'd made her do that. He felt like the fuckin' king of the world right now. "Everyone was staring and laughing, and I couldn't pick it back up without looking like a weirdo, so I had to leave it on the table in the restaurant. It was just about the hardest thing I've ever done in my life."

"And then today I gave you a present."

Face stretching into a smile, he nodded. She got it. She got where he was going with this without him having to say anything else. Eden was a smart girl. It made him happy and sad at the same time. She saw deeper than he expected her to, but it also meant she would leave him sooner. Smart girls didn't fall for broken boys like him.

Eden was getting shy as they walked through the woods toward the Red Havoc cabins. He could tell because she kept looking down at her shoes in between the times she braved looking him directly in the eyes. And her smile was different. It was steady and sweet, and she kept letting her hair fall forward in front of her face as if she wanted to hide that pretty color on her cheeks from him. He didn't like that, so he reached over and tucked the wavy strands behind her ear. Shocking him to his core, she grabbed his hand and squeezed. And just as he thought she would let go, she intertwined their fingers and held his hand like she didn't mind the oil that clung to him from working in the shop. Or the rough callouses on his palm, or the disproportionate size, which was way bigger than her petite hands. He made sure to keep his grip extra gentle so he wouldn't crush her bones to dust. He'd always been too big and rough, but Eden deserved the effort not to accidentally squish her like a grape. Out of all the people on Earth, he wanted to murder her the least.

Just touching her settled the tension that constantly zinged through his body. She was warm, funny, and normal, and for the first time in his life, he wished he could've survived what happened to the Four Deadlies. He hadn't, though. The boy he was had died, and in his place a monster had been born. And now he was full of regrets because a pretty girl like Eden, who made his heart pound and his dick throb and his head orbit around her, deserved better than what he'd become. He'd become survival. She needed a steady man.

"What do you do for fun?" she asked.

A lady like Eden probably wouldn't appreciate the answer "Kill shit," so he gave her a second-place response. "Making moonshine is fun. It's challenging, kind of like chemistry, and the extra income doesn't suck." Plus making the real hooch wasn't exactly legal so that made it even more fun.

"Only one hobby, Barret?"

He shrugged. "I run the auto shop and, outside of

that, trying not to kick my crew's ass on a daily basis is a full-time job."

"Well I have billions of hobbies, so are you ready to be wowed by my rich life?"

Silly bird. He was wowed by literally everything she said. She didn't even have to try. "Wow me."

"First of all, I'm pretty good with construction paper…" Her voice faded as his ears pricked at the sound of the Red Havoc Crew.

Could she hear them? Eden showed no sign of noticing the argument that had broken out between Anson and Jaxon over a hockey game that had been played last week. Idiots. They were so fuckin' loud and they were taking away from Eden's words right now. She spoke on like she couldn't hear them, and he thought maybe snowy owls couldn't hear well like big cat shifters. Her lips were pretty when they shaped words. She enunciated well, like smart girls did.

Damn, it was hot out here. He tugged at his shirt to let air hit his stomach. She was talking about her hobbies—crocheting, yoga, and brewing her own small batches of beer in her garage. So fucking cute. And normal. There was a hundred percent chance he would fuck this up. Why was it so hot out here? Maybe he should Change. *No. Be cool.*

"And the hops are what make the beer…" Eden rambled. She was nervous. Her hand was shaking in his, and he didn't like that.

She'd been hurt before…rejected by that chode-hair who didn't want her touching him. What the fuck was his name? Marcus. That dickweevil deserved a fiery death. Eden was beautiful. Her platinum blond hair lifted at the ends in the wind, shining in the sun like a ptarmigan's feather in winter. Her eyes were more gray than blue today, but not just a single shade. They were darker in the middles and went lighter, branching out with subtle color changes. From farther away, they were the shade of storm clouds, but right here, they were more like the shiny silver back of a minnow in a stream. He wished she would look at him longer so he could memorize the tiny details in the color of her eyes.

Why was she shaking? When a shadow passed overhead, she hunched and glanced up so fast she was a blur, showing her shifter speed. For a split second, there was fear in her eyes, which had turned a striking silver color in an instant. A snarl rattled up his throat as he watched the hawk above them, floating lazily on the wind currents, probably searching the forest floor for dinner.

Eden was squeezing his hand hard, and she smelled faintly of terror. He couldn't help himself and pulled her against his side, draped his arm over her shoulder, still holding her hand right over her chest.

"You're safe here." He said it like she was safe in Red Havoc territory, but really, he meant she was safe with him. Like all the dumbasses in his crew, he would protect her just the same. If they got his fealty, this woman got his utter devotion and the protection of his body as long as she stayed here.

Eden let off this little sigh...this soft, cute, tiny, fucking boner-inducing sigh as though she believed him. And then, like he was a man and not a monster, she rested her cheek against his chest as they walked.

He'd done it. He'd tricked the smart girl.

He wanted to trick her forever because he'd never felt a connection like this. He bet her snowy owl was gorgeous, just like her human side. He imagined his green-eyed panther walking under a massive snowy owl, her wings outstretched, bathing him in her shadow from above, catching wind currents like that hawk had.

"You're slowing down," Eden pointed out.

Smart girl saw too much, saw everything but the monster, so he admitted, "I don't want to go back yet. I'll have to pretend I don't want to fuck you in front of them."

Eden eased back and looked up at him. Her full lips were puckered in the cutest fucking little frown he'd ever seen. "Why?"

"Because they'll read too much into it." And give him shit for the rest of his life. "And it's none of their damn business."

Now her frown was deepening, making little lines around her mouth. She eased out from under his arm and walked away into the clearing in front of the Red Havoc cabins. She wasn't even shaking her ass for him as she walked.

Confused, Barret stood there with his arms out, palms up. "What's wrong?"

"Nothing," Eden said over her shoulder. She didn't slow at all. "I'm fine."

Ew. Those two words made his stomach curdle, but he couldn't figure out why. Okaaay, if she said she was fine, she was fine. Crisis averted and shit.

Barret followed after her, but she sped up, which only spurred on his primal instinct to chase her like she was prey. Fucking sexy prey that he wanted to eat. Out. That he wanted to eat out. He pushed his legs into a speed walk, but she tossed him a challenging look over her shoulder and started jogging toward where the crew was sitting around a bonfire. Why was chasing after her turning him on right now?

They both skidded to a stop near the fire. Everyone was staring at them with matching scowls.

Anson asked, "Who are you, and why the fuck is Murder Kitty chasing you?"

His boy, Bentley, sang, "Anson said fuck for the third time todaaaaay."

"Boy, are you counting? And don't say fuck!"

"Four," Bentley announced.

His mother, Kaylee, snorted and tried to keep a stern face as she laid into her son for saying "fuck." Jaxon was lying on the ground where his mate Annalise, aka the psychotic panther named She-Devil, sat feeding him grapes like a cabana boy. The Red Havoc Crew alpha, Ben, was flipping ears of corn on the grill while his mate Jenny had her hand in his back pocket and was whispering something probably perverted-as-fuck into his ear. And Raif, their son, just threw a bug into the fire. Or a booger. Barret couldn't tell from here. At least Greyson wasn't here. He wanted to kick that dick-pimple in the taint most days. He'd been a grumpy beast of a shifter lately, and it made Barret want to kill him. Not Barret's fault. Greyson's.

Why was everyone staring at him? Even Eden. God, her lips and hips were distracting. He couldn't decide which one he wanted more on his dick right now.

"Dude, do you have a boner?" Jaxon asked, lifting into a crunch position as his mate settled her legs under his head.

"Probably. She's hot. Why are you looking at my dick, LVP?" Barret retorted.

"Stop calling me that," Jaxon snarled. "I'm not the least valuable player. You are."

"You're getting fed grapes by a lunatic like you can't even feed your grown-ass self. L. V. P."

Eden let off the tiniest giggle and then pursed her lips. She cleared her throat and asked, "Are you going to introduce me to everyone?"

Barret looked around at everyone's stupid, expectant faces. "No, why?"

"You would be waiting your whole life for those introductions," Kaylee said in a tired voice. "He has no manners. I'm Kaylee, this is Jenny and Annalise…" She went around the circle introducing everyone. Snore. "You obviously know the resident Barret the Barbarian."

When Annalise and Jenny laughed, Barret wanted to throw dirt, glass shards, and dung beetles in their fruity beers to punish them. Girls were so annoying. Except for Eden. She was funny and sexy and tough and she wore red bras and she did a siren song for his dick that called it to attention every thirty seconds and made him feel like a pervert and he liked her a lot. He wanted to touch her. Just a little touch to settle his annoyance with the village idiots in his crew. Just a little brush of her back. There. He stroked his fingers down her spine, and her face went completely slack as a tremble worked its way up her body, growing bigger and bigger until it landed in her shoulders and she gave off a soft, sexy noise. Were her pupils dilated? Now he was annoyed that the crew even existed because he wanted to bend her over that empty pink lawn chair by the bonfire and fuck her relentlessly until she was screaming his name.

"Barret!" Ben barked out.

He ripped his gaze away from Eden's treasure box. "Huh, what?"

Ben was staring at Barret like he'd lost his mind. "What the fuck is wrong with you?"

"I think you mean what the fuck is right with me. That answer would be 'everything.'"

Eden gave a single laugh that was so loud it echoed across the clearing, but immediately clapped her hand over her mouth. Her eyes were dancing though, so Barret could tell she was still grinning. He liked making her smile, but he couldn't figure out why she found him so damn amusing. None of the Red Havoc crew ever laughed at how hilarious he was. Eden, apparently, had a sense of humor that matched his own. *Ten more sexy points go to her.*

Eden cleared her throat and spoke up through her still lingering smile. "I'm Eden, and Lynn invited me here. I'm staying with her for a while until she recovers."

"Recovers?" Anson asked. "I've seen zero

improvement from the time her deadbeat mate left until now. She tries to literally kill me any time I'm within two hundred yards of her hermit tree."

"It's a *tree house*," Eden said, stubbornness tingeing her voice.

He liked how protective Eden was over Lynn, but Barret didn't like when she was upset and grew suddenly desperate to turn her darkening mood around. "I'm gonna feed you my meat."

"That's a gross way to put it, Barret," Jenny reprimanded him.

Barret shrugged. "I bought the ribs. My meat."

Jenny jammed a finger at Barret and looked utterly baffled when she asked Eden, "Do you like him? Like…is *that* your thing? He's level-red-weird. I'm concerned."

"Uuuuh…" Eden murmured, eyes wide.

"She totally likes him," Anson said. "Look, she's not even flinching away from him and he's been petting her like she's a stray cat for five minutes."

Barret stopped stroking down her spine. Oops. He hadn't realized he was still doing that.

"Smells like pheromones," Jaxon said around a mouthful of grapes from where his head lay in

Annalise's lap. "Good to see you again, Duckie."

Eden scrunched up her face. "Don't call me that, or I'll bring up all your childhood nicknames, *Wormy-Toot-Toot*."

The Gray Back grizzly shifter threw up his hands in surrender, but he was still smiling. For some reason, Barret wanted to kill him, as usual.

"You're from Damon's Mountains?" Ben asked.

"That I am. I work for Damon, actually. He's my boss."

"Well that's fucking terrifying," Anson muttered. "We want zero trouble with the blue dragon."

"Aw, he's not so scary," Eden said with a wink at Jaxon.

Jaxon pointed at her and said promptly, "Lie. He's a people eater. I've seen him devour ashes so many times I would rather chew my own arm off than cross him. Duckie here just sees the good in everyone. It's annoying actually."

"Take that back," Barret growled. *She's perfect.* He wanted to say that so bad, but Eden would run away if she discovered how infatuated he already was with her. God, his panther wanted to claw out of his skin and bleed Jaxon just for calling her annoying.

"Take what back?" Jaxon asked, lifting his head to glare at Barret.

"Call her names, and I'll rip your innards through your mouth hole. Take. It. Back."

Jaxon sighed and plopped his head back into Annalise's lap, then opened his mouth like a baby bird waiting to be fed. She dropped a grape into his gaping maw. Barret viciously fought the urge to kick him in his stupid Gray Back dick and make him choke on the fruit.

Jaxon chewed with his mouth open, smacking loudly. "Fine. I take it back."

From the shadows of the nearest cabin, Greyson asked, "Why do they call you Duckie?"

Barret was used to Greyson pretending he was a damn ghost and hiding in dark corners so he wasn't startled, but Eden jumped hard.

God, he just wanted to touch her! He wanted to reassure her she was safe with him, but everyone was staring like he and Eden were the main act of a circus, and the crew was already giving them shit, and he hated everyone but Eden. And Bentley and Raif, who were now playing on the edge of the woods. Jaxon had his knees bent and spread where he lay, and Barret had to clench his fists to fight the still chronic urge to dick-kick him. Eden kept looking at the sky, setting his panther on edge, and Ben was burning the corn. When Eden began shifting her weight from side to side as if she didn't want to answer the question, Barret got dizzy with the urge to Change.

"Because when she was a kid," Jaxon volunteered, "she followed all of us around like a little baby duck. But she never wanted to play or join in on the fun."

Eden arched her perfect, pretty, delicate eyebrows up to nearly her hairline. "Fun being spin the bottle in Beaston's tree house and taking shots of your dad's Fireball whiskey before Changing drunk and bleeding each other? No spanks."

"See?" Jaxon rumbled, sitting up and puffing out his chest. "Boring *and* annoying." A challenge flashed in his eyes, which had lightened to an inhuman green. Smiling at Barret, Jaxon was testing him, asking for a fight.

Well, okay Gray Back.

Wish. Fucking. Granted.

SEVEN

"No, no, no, no!" Jenny screamed as Barret ripped apart in an instant.

Eden barely had time to get out of the way before the massive pure-black panther charged Jaxon. Oh, she'd seen Jaxon's grizzly growing up. He was a beast, but Barret's panther was terrifying. He was damn near the size of a mature male lion, three times the size of a panther in the wild, and his face was twisted in a fearsome expression that promised death to Jaxon's grizzly. And he was fast. So fast. She pitched backward out of the way, and just before she hit the ground and put her tailbone through her esophagus, Barret changed course and skidded under her, cushioning her fall.

There was a moment when she thought, *well, that was sweet. He pulled off mid-fight to make sure I was okay. Swoon.* And then she'd seen Jaxon barreling toward her with murder in his glowing green eyes, and adrenaline had dumped into her system. Change, Change, Change, Change! The falcon was quiet inside of her, watching, uninterested in fucking survival, apparently, because she wasn't answering Eden's desperate call. She needed her wings, but the falcon didn't give them to her.

Barret slid out from under her and stood over her body as she curled in on herself and waited for a monstrous swat from Jaxon's brown bear. Barret's body jerked, and a panther scream ripped through the night. Then his weight was gone.

She was afraid to open her eyes. What if he had been blasted all the way across the clearing, or was injured so badly he couldn't come back from it? But when she did find her courage and ease one eye open, it was Jaxon who was in trouble. Barret was latched onto his neck, jaws working, every claw dug into Jaxon's thick skin as he held himself in place for that kill bite.

"Barret, stop!" Ben yelled as the massive grizzly

ripped desperately at Barret's back. Claw mark after claw mark showed up crimson against Barret's black fur as Jaxon roared his fury and pain.

Falcon! I need you!

She had to do something to help, but she just sat there instead. Who was she supposed to defend? Her childhood friend or the man who had somehow pulled her heart from her chest and claimed it like a goddamned wizard?

The others were Changing now. Ben's massive black cat hit Barret so hard his left paw raked down Jaxon's shoulder. Ben sank his teeth into Barret's shoulder, but Murder Kitty didn't even flinch. It was as if he felt no pain at all.

Jaxon and Barret were destroying everything like a hurricane. Dirt was kicked up in a cloud as they spun and battled. They crashed through chairs and then through the grill, meat and corn cobs flying into the air, the screech of metal piercing the peaceful night. Jenny was yelling at Annalise not to Change, but it was too late. She was doubled over, teeth too long at the canines, eyes shining in the dim light like an animal's in headlights. And strangely enough, in this moment of clarity, fear, and confusion, Eden realized those shining eyes were intent on her.

A black panther with charcoal-gray spots through her coat exploded from Annalise and immediately charged.

"Fuck!" Jenny yelled. "Eden, run!"

Run? She needed to fly! Fly away from this crew of unbalanced crazy-cats. She'd grown up with the Ashe Crew, but Red Havoc was even worse in their violent tendencies.

"Oh, my gosh," Eden murmured as she rolled out of the path of the three panthers trying to separate Jaxon and Barret.

They cut off her line of sight to Annalise's cat, but Eden had seen the look of a hunter before, and Annalise wouldn't be put off for long. Eden pushed up and sprinted as fast as she could toward the closest cabin. Each step was agony because she knew she was being chased by a terrifying shifter—one who would hurt her badly if she caught her.

Stairs, stairs, stairs, so close. She just had to make it to the stairs, across the small porch, and in through the door. Please God let it be unlocked! She could feel the beast so close behind her. No time to turn around and gauge how much time she had. The answer was no time at all.

The instant her hand touched the door handle, something massive barreled into her and slammed her against the door. Pain slashed across the front of her right thigh, and she yelled out in agony as she hit the ground. The spotted panther looked over her shoulder for an instant before she screamed a deafening sound, opened her mouth, and came for Eden's throat.

A black torpedo hit her with the power of a Mack truck. Annalise went straight through the railing, destroying half the porch on impact. And then Barret was there, protecting her body as Eden rolled back and forth on her back in pain, gripping her shredded thigh. The scent of iron filled the air. Her blood painted the porch, and when she looked around Barret's massive body, her heart threatened to pound right out of her chest. Jaxon was stalking them, his throat torn to pieces and streaming crimson. The panthers were approaching too, and so was an enormous, muscular lioness. All of their ears were flattened against their heads, teeth bared, bloodlust in their eyes, and she was in trouble. No, not just her. She and Barret were both in trouble because he wasn't backing down an inch. He let off a deep scream and raked his claws across the face of the nearest panther who got too close. The change in the animal's facial expression was instant. He lurched back, unsnarled his lips and looked around at the others, like he didn't know how he'd gotten here. Bloodlust did that to predator shifters. It took over the mind.

Barret went after that panther again with another paw to the face. The slap echoed across the clearing, and then Barret was back to her, standing over her, protecting her. His tail was twitching with agitation, but whatever he was doing to the big panther, it seemed to be working.

The predator turned on the lioness and hissed long and low. God, his teeth were so long. These males were mature, dominant, and were much bigger than Lynn's panther. He hissed again, the sound tapering into a low growl. The sound turned to a groan when the panther tucked away and Ben's human skin replaced it. "Change back!" he demanded. "Now!"

Even Eden who wasn't a part of this crew could feel the power behind his order. Barret wasn't

Changing, but the others were affected immediately. Their Changes looked forced and painful. They were slow, and there was a chorus of agonized groans while their bodies broke apart.

Clutching her leg to staunch the bleeding, Eden sat up slowly, carefully. Barret turned around, and she was stunned by the vibrant color of his green eyes. She'd never seen a green-eyed panther before, and the color was striking against the pitch color of his fur. His pupils were so small his eyes looked even brighter as he scanned her body. He didn't seem to see the others as a threat anymore since he gave his crew his back. Barret leaned down and sniffed at her hands, which were smeared with red.

He nudged her hands to the side gently and ran his tongue up the tattered fabric of her jeans. It hurt so bad, but when she tried to shield it from him again, he hissed a warning.

"Give them space," Ben ordered, jerking his chin toward the destroyed chairs and grill. His crew followed him and then began righting chairs and picking food off the ground, murmuring softly to each other, too low for Eden to hear.

Her leg hurt less now. It was her shifter healing

kicking in, but falcons didn't heal as fast as other shifters. She would probably have claw mark scars thanks to Annalise, and the adrenaline dump was making her shake badly, but Barret seemed intent on cleaning her. He laid on his belly, half across her legs, and laved his tongue across her claw mark over and over until she stopped bleeding entirely. A purr rattled his wrecked body. She had one claw mark. He had dozens. He'd already stopped bleeding, but most of them were open and painful looking.

He was hurt, yet here he was taking care of her in his own animalistic way.

With a sigh to release some of the tension, she eased back against the door and brushed her fingers lightly over his ear as he worked. Her chest felt all strange and fluttery, and with each slow lick of his tongue, she found more courage to pet him deeper. Palm flat, she ran it up his massive head. Barret closed his eyes as he cleaned her, as if her touch felt good. Oh, she liked him. He was as violent as a Gray Back, broken perhaps, but he'd come for her twice in one fight. Come to protect her. And she'd seen him. Felt him. He would've gone to war with his entire damn crew to protect her.

Who was this man who was collecting her devotion so seamlessly? Barret seemed to have so many walls and barriers, but his panther was clearly just fine in letting her see his caring side.

He stood suddenly and meandered gracefully off the porch where Annalise had broken the rails. She was in Jaxon's arms near the doused bonfire, talking low and swaying with him. He had one arm around her, the other hand gripping his neck where he was still bleeding. And it struck her what Annalise had done. The others had been struggling to get Barret off her mate, so she'd gone after Eden instead of Barret. Clever cat. She'd taken a risk and left her mate vulnerable to get Barret's attention off Jaxon. She'd attacked Eden, and Barret had come for her.

But what did it mean that Annalise knew going after Eden would work? What did it mean that it did work? What did it mean that Barret could be pulled off a kill bite, in full-blown bloodlust, and come to protect her instead?

Mate.

She shook her head slowly because that couldn't be right. She couldn't hold a man's attention. She wasn't meant for a mate, and Barret had said the same thing about himself.

Mate.

Her falcon was finally here, just in time to whisper that one, all-important word inside of her.

Could he be the one she'd waited for her whole life?

Could he be the one to end the loneliness?

Don't fall in love.

Barret strode out of the shadows, his eyes burning right into her. His big fists were clenched, and his strides were long and powerful. His naked body was the epitome of masculinity and predatory grace. He was smeared with blood and dirt, and his eyes were intense, locked on hers with such intensity, she couldn't take her eyes away from him if she wanted to.

He was coming straight for her. Something deep inside of her said he was the type of man who would protect her at all costs to him.

It wasn't L-O-V-E yet, but in that moment, she reached the second letter.

Barret didn't slow as he approached. He simply hopped the three stairs gracefully and stooped, picked her up like she weighed nothing, gathered her tightly to his chest, and then shoved open the door to the cabin.

"Is this…is this your den?" she asked quietly as she looked around the small living room.

"Yes," he said in a voice that was low and gravelly. And sexy.

The couch and chair were made of dark, fragrant leather, and on the rustic wooden coffee table, there were outdoor magazines in disarray. Two pair of work boots, covered in dirt and scuffs, sat by the front door. A tan jacket hung on a hook on the wall along with a set of keys, and the kitchen across the living room was small but tidy, other than a sink full of dishes.

"I should've stayed away longer," he said low, settling her on her feet. He gripped her hips, rested his forehead against hers, closed his eyes, and inhaled deeply. "I want you rough right now, *so* bad."

She inhaled sharply at what those words did to her body. He made her instantly wet, instantly ready for him. Her nipples drew up to tight buds, like they were begging for him to suck on them. Rough didn't sound like a bad idea at all right now. Perhaps those five words would've scared her with anyone else, but with Barret, they were a huge turn-on. Especially with him backing her toward the bedroom off the kitchen. Especially with his fingers digging into her hips. Especially with his thick erection pressed against her belly. She wanted him inside her, and right now, after the adrenaline rush and the fear and the realization of how damn important he was…she wanted him to be himself and take her as he pleased.

He leaned down and kissed her, but his breath shook. He was too controlled. He was fighting his nature to keep gentle.

"No, Bad Cat," she whispered. "No hiding tonight." She kissed him and bit his bottom lip almost hard enough to draw blood.

Cut up, smelling like iron and fur, Barret snarled and yanked her hips against his as he kissed her again. This time he let his control slip and thrust his tongue into her mouth immediately. And each time he dominated her mouth, he let off a quick breath and rocked his hips against her hard.

She was already so wet from the anticipation that when he pushed his hand down into her panties and shoved a finger inside of her, she was ready. Eden groaned when he pulled it out slowly and licked his finger. "I fucking love the way you taste, Eden."

His hand gripped her hair at the base of her neck as her ass hit a dresser. It was dark in here, but her eyes were adjusting. Another kiss, harder this time, and he was controlling the pace. Sexy, sexy man. She didn't like to be bossed around in the outside world, but here, with the man she trusted, she wanted him to show her what he liked. She wanted him to take control and instruct her on what to do.

"Turn around," he murmured.

Okay then, hell yes, she was ready to do this! Until the point when she saw herself in the mirror and realized she was going to have to watch herself *do this*.

"Watch *me*," he said as he peeled her shirt over her head. "I'm about to fuck the shit out of you, Eden, but you'll know it isn't casual for me. *You* aren't casual for me. I need fast and hard right now, but I'll take care of you better our second time."

Oooh, he was already making plans for next time?

Ziiiip. The sound of her zipper wrenched a helpless noise from her throat. Arching her back, she rolled her ass against his erection and exhaled breathily when his hand went to her throat, the other to her hip. He drew her back against him tightly. He was so hard and so thick.

"I fucking love the way you react to me," he murmured in that sexy, deep tone of his.

Her panties tickled her knees on the way down, and when Barret pushed them to her ankles, she stepped out of them and kicked them into the pile with the other clothes. She liked how Barret didn't hesitate on removing her clothes. She didn't have to question if he wanted her, not like with Marcus. His lips touched her shoulder blade at the exact same moment he grabbed her hip and pulled her back against his dick. She gasped at the fiery sensation of his soft bite. With each sucking kiss that his teeth scraped her skin, she rolled back against him in a steady rhythm, begging silently for him to be inside of her already.

He brushed his fingertips down her arm, intertwined their fingers, then slammed her hand on the dresser, held it there tightly as he shoved her ankles farther apart. Please, please, please. God she was so ready. He was right there at her entrance. As Barret pushed into her by a couple inches, he growled out a sexy sound. She groaned his name and rolled her eyes closed. This had to be better than the best high. He withdrew, and the next time he wasn't gentle. After a moment of hesitation, he slammed into her. So deep. Soooo deep. She arched her back, giving him a better angle, begging for more. Begging for it all.

He pulled back and thrust into her again, his hand still clutching hers, pinning hers to the dresser. His other hand held her hips in place, setting the pace, pulling her onto his dick as he pushed into her again and again, faster now. Faster and harder until she could hear the rhythmic slap of their skin. Until she was filled to bursting and moaning with how good it felt. Until his hand went to her hair, pulled it in the back, made her arch her spine even deeper as he pummeled into her.

She'd never finished like this, not even close, but orgasm exploded through her unexpectedly. It felt so intensely good, all she could do was cry out his name and grip where his hand pinned hers. She opened her eyes just in time to see him grit his teeth, blazing green eyes on hers in their reflection, his powerful body slamming into her one last time before he yelled out and froze. Warmth spurted into her, and then he moved again, sliding in and out of her with each pulse of his release. Warmth trickled down her legs, but he didn't stop until both of their throbbing orgasms had slowed and eventually faded to nothing.

His hand went gentle in her hair, and he ran the flat of his palm down her back, eyes raking hungrily over her body in the mirror. The way he looked at her made her feel like a goddess.

"You're beautiful," he murmured and pressed a kiss against the tip of her shoulder, eyes on hers in the mirror. "I have to tell you something. Something bad."

"Tell me anything," she whispered.

"I wanted to bite you. You'll have to be careful giving me your back now. I was close to claiming you, and trust me Eden, you don't want that kind of devotion from me."

She couldn't help but feel hurt. "Why not?"

He bit her shoulder gently, held the skin there between his teeth. The corners of his lips lifted in a feral smile. Releasing her, he said, "Because I'll ruin your life. I'm on my way down a bunny hole, and I can't turn around. You don't want me taking you with me." The corners of his eyes tightened slightly, and the smile dipped from his face so fast it was as if it had never existed at all. "Trust me."

Eden turned slowly and slipped her arms around his back, rested her cheek against his chest, and sighed. "Wall."

"What?"

"You put up walls, but you tease me. You show me the good parts of you for just a second, and then you cover it back up again. I still see you though, Barret."

His heart drummed under her cheek. In a voice so low she almost missed it, he murmured, "Say that again."

She scratched her nails gently up his back, raising gooseflesh with her touch. "I. See. You."

He exhaled a gust of trembling breath, as if he'd been holding it in his whole life. His muscles relaxed under her touch, and he slid his arms around her, hugged her so tight it was hard to breathe, but she didn't care. Barret was jokes and loudness to distract from the gritty parts of himself he didn't want people to notice. He hadn't been careful enough with her though, and she saw the rough edges. She saw, and she accepted them.

He was smoke and mirrors, but the real Barret,

the complicated parts of him, were ready for violence. A part of him seemed to need it. He was a dangerous man to mess with, one who didn't back down an inch, and though she realized it and saw him for what he was, she'd been on the other end of that tonight. She'd been curled in a ball, bleeding, hurt, defenseless when her falcon abandoned her, but Barret hadn't left her. He'd stood over her, ready to face down every monster in his crew to keep her body safe.

He might be dangerous to others who crossed him. But down to her soul, she knew he wouldn't hurt her. She was safe. God, that feeling of safety was so hard for her to accept, but right now, in his strong arms, the warmth of it blanketed and soothed her. With Barret, she was safe from his crew, safe from the falcons that would come for her someday, safe from loneliness.

She was beginning to understand his walls, and the thing about that was…the more she studied them, the more transparent they became.

It wasn't L-O-V-E yet, but she'd just arrived at the letter V.

EIGHT

"Okay, our options are limited," Barret announced in a business voice as he strode back into the bedroom looking like a tall glass of lemonade on a southern August night.

She was trying to focus on the problem of dinner, but he was sans shirt, wearing only jeans that sat low enough to expose the muscular V-muscles over his hips. Eight. She counted eight abs by twos, and each set was perfectly symmetrical, sitting in the shadow of his perfectly defined pecs and perfectly drawn-up nipples. In this light, from where she sat on his bed cuddling a pillow in her lap, she could see his tattoo clearly.

Her heart sank as she realized what the bird was.

It was a falcon. One like her but with brown feathers with tan stripes, patterned like the Welkin Raiders. There were tattooed marks beneath one of the talons. Small, straight lines neatly placed one after the other. The deaths of his crew? His people? Had he really marked the losses and blows he'd been dealt?

Barret covered the tattoo encircling his shoulder with his hand, and when she dragged her attention to his face, his expression was somber. He shook his head. "I don't like when you look at that part of me."

"You mean the most important part? The part that made you the man you are?"

He huffed a humorless laugh, then shook his head hard. "Don't like it," he murmured in a strange voice. "Food. I'm gonna get us food. Stop looking, Eden." His head ticked, a slight jerk to the right, and he murmured, "Fuck." Stooping, he yanked a shirt off the floor and then pulled it over his head in a rush as he left the room.

She should tell him what she was.

It felt wrong to hide her shifter animal, but now she was scared. Not of Barret, but of losing him. He didn't even want her to look at his falcon tattoo. How would he react if he knew he'd just slept with one?

Eden wasn't a part of the falcons. Never had been. Mom had kept her safe and tucked away in Damon's Mountains. She told her horrible stories about the falcons and their war. Eden had never met her grandfather, or any other falcons other than Mom, but would Barret forgive her for the bird inside of her?

She was too cowardly to find out because she wanted to keep him. And she didn't care what that said about her. They were growing something big—something important. She would tell him when she was sure he was in this and wouldn't run.

Eden took one of his oversize T-shirts from the bottom drawer and pulled it on as she padded into the kitchen where he was gathering piles of random food onto a tray—cheese crackers, squeeze cheese, peanut butter, lunch meat, strawberries, blackberries, granola bars, two chocolate chip muffins, one jar of olives, and a jar of raspberry jelly. He shoved a bowl filled with crunched-up chocolate bar pieces into the microwave.

"The meat is on the ground and covered in dirt. I blame that on that Jax-hole grizzly. Freaking dinnerruiner."

It was a subject change to escape the deep conversation they'd been having in the bedroom. "Barret," she said softly.

"I mean, I would still eat it, but for you, Mud ala Grass Clippings isn't the best flavor," he said without turning around.

God, she wanted to hug him. She wanted to wrap her arms around him from behind. She hated him being so bright and cheerful, knowing he was purposefully hiding that tattoo from her and hurting in ways she couldn't understand because he'd erected yet another wall. She wanted to hold him until the obvious tension in every muscle in his back eased. Until he relaxed against her and spilled his secrets, just so she could shoulder the burdens with him, but he wouldn't do that. He was like one of those flowers that bloomed only once every several years. Patience was required.

Oh, she could ask Mom or Damon Daye exactly what happened to the Four Deadlies Crew all those years ago. Mom kept watch on the falcons from the outside, and Damon watched all shifters. But it didn't feel right to steal Barret's story. It would mean more to them both if he gave it to her freely when he was ready.

Eden hopped up on the counter. "Favorite color?"

"Red like that bra you wore at the grocery store."

Eden laughed. "Really?"

"Yes, really. Are we playing twenty questions?"

"Yeah, I figured I should get to know the man I'm sleeping with."

"Mmm, you mean fucking. You'll know when I'm sleeping with you. Tonight, I was too rough. I'm always too rough."

"I'm not fragile," she said low, gripping the edge of the counter on either side of her legs.

"Aren't you?" Barret turned around, and his eyes were too bright, as if his panther was right under his surface. He was still upset about her staring at the tattoo. "You're submissive."

"But tough. I had to be where I'm from. Submissive doesn't mean weak in Damon's Mountains. Crews need submissives just like we need dominants. I helped balance the Ashe Crew for my whole life."

"Fine-boned snowy owl, I could eat you in one bite."

"You have eaten me, and I'm still here," she said, waggling her eyebrows. Yep, she was definitely ignoring the snowy owl comment.

He laughed, a genuine one, and yanked the melted chocolate from the microwave, then settled between her legs, setting the tray of random snacks beside her. He dipped a strawberry in the melted dark chocolate and fed it to her without missing a beat, then ate what she didn't bite off. "My favorite color used to be gray."

"Gray? That's hella boring."

He snickered and dipped a blackberry in the chocolate. "You say boring, but I liked gray because it was the color of storm clouds. When I was a kid, I had a step-mom, Marney. She was amazing. Fuck." His head jerked over and over, like he was stuck in a twitch. In a strained voice he said, "It's okay. It's okay. You'll keep this safe, right Eden?"

Eden cupped his cheeks, and the twitching stopped. Face angled to the side, he flicked his gaze to hers. He looked lost, and it pulled at her heart. "I'll keep everything you give me safe," she promised in a clear tone so he could hear the honest inflections of every word.

"Marney liked stormy days best. She would take me to this coffee shop in town, early in the morning on rainy days, because she said it had the best window for watching raindrop races. We would sit in her favorite place, this booth in the corner right by the big picture window on the front wall of this little café. I would drink hot chocolate, and she would drink coffee black, and we would watch the raindrop races. Fuck. Fuck." *Twitch. Twitch.*

Eden leaned forward and kissed his lips quick, held his cheeks in place until he relaxed and stopped the jerky movement. He let off a shaky breath. "I don't scratch at these memories for a reason. I know you want answers, but I can't give them to you."

"Can I have one?"

Barret wouldn't meet her eyes, but after a minute, he nodded once. "One."

"What kind of shifter was Marney?" Oh, she had an idea, but she was hoping and praying she was wrong.

"Falcon," he croaked out. "She's the one in the tattoo. Fuck." His shoulders jerked up to his ears, and before he turned away, she could see the bone-deep pain in his eyes. The sadness. It gutted her.

Oh she could guess exactly what happened. Marney was a female falcon who had escaped her people, and been looking for sanctuary. She'd fallen for Barret's father, but her love had gotten the entire Four Deadlies Crew murdered. All but her stepson.

Chills rippled across Eden's skin. She hated the falcons. Hated what she was, hated the blood that ran through her veins, hated everything about her lineage on her mother's side. She'd wished so many times over the years to be like the other kids in the Ashe Crew—to Change with them and walk among them on the ground in the woods, not flying above, alone. She'd hated her white feathers, because they kept her in even more danger from the falcons. She'd wished her uniqueness away in weak moments, but right now, she would do just about anything to go back and be born a fearsome grizzly shifter like her dad. There was honor among the grizzlies, and none among the falcons. Mom had said that a dozen times when she explained why they lived in a grizzly crew instead of with other flight shifters.

Desperate to turn her dark thoughts around, she said, "My favorite color is purple, but I don't have any cool stories to go with it. I just like grapes."

Barret snorted, and the heavy look in his eyes lifted. "Maybe Jaxon was right."

"About what?"

"About you being boring."

He laughed and jerked out of swatting range. She'd wanted to really smack him, and with the miss, she got off-balance and lurched forward off the counter. Right before she caught the ground with her face, Barret pulled her up.

Now, he was laughing really hard. "And clumsy."

Eden glared and gave a sarcastic, "My hero," before she yanked out of his arms and dipped a blackberry in chocolate and ate it. And then she ate another and another. "I hope these are your favorite snack," she said around a full mouth. "I'm going to eat them all."

"Those are my least favorite snack," he said with a smirk, crossing his arms over his chest.

She tried strawberries next, but he only shook his head. It wasn't lunch meat, chocolate chip muffins, or granola bars either.

"My stomach hurts," she whined, wrapping her arms around her middle.

Barret belted out a laugh and grabbed the cheese

crackers off the counter. And then he did something appallingly disgusting.

"Are you seriously dipping cheese crackers in peanut butter?"

"Stop judging me," he said, crunching away on a bite. "I'm an emotional eater, and I discovered this while watching reruns of old cooking shows."

Voice pitched high, she asked, "You were watching them cook real food, and you were making this monstrosity?"

Smiling, he dipped the next one in peanut butter, then raspberry jelly. Gag.

"Barret, don't put that in your mouth."

Crunch.

"Oooh, my tummy really hurts," she muttered. "And you're gross."

"Try it."

"No!"

"Try it, Eden. Stop being boring. Here, I'll cook it for you." He dipped the cracker in PB&J and shoved it at her. "Let me feed you like a helpless baby bird, just like Jaxon Wormy Toot Toot, or whatever you called him. It'll be romantic. We'll be so cute and gross everyone out with how good we are at romance."

Eden scrunched up her face. "Jaxon had grapes to eat, not gross stuff."

"Eat it, and I'll let you suck my dick."

She was trying so hard not to laugh right now. "That's literally the worst negotiation I've ever heard."

Barret was cracking up, but trying to keep a straight face as he hovered the horrid little hors d'oeuvres in front of her face, flying it like a plane, just like parents did with toddlers.

She ate it, but to spite him, she bit the shit out of his finger.

"Didn't hurt! Turned me on instead," he punched out through his laughter.

"Oh, my God, you really have a boner," she exclaimed, pointing at the front of his jeans where, indeed, there was a big bulge.

"Uhhh, everything you do turns me on."

"Challenge considered. Challenge accepted." Eden raised the squeeze cheese to her mouth and hesitated, arching her eyebrow primly. And then she squirted the liquid cheddar in her maw and smiled really big.

"You look so fucking sexy with yellow teeth. Let's

cheese-kiss."

"Ew," she said, snickering. She tried to swallow as fast as she could before he got the brilliant idea to actually kiss her.

"Dick's still hard," he announced. "Let's go swimming."

"Swimming? Where? And it's too cold out, so no thanks. I need to get back to Lynn anyway."

"Lynn survived just fine for like a dozen months before you came along. She's okay. She'll be just as steadily crazy when you go back to her in the morning. Tonight, you're mine, and I want to go swimming." He hooked his hands on his hips. "Naked. Bring the cheese."

"I've never been skinny-dipping."

"Ever in your life?" He sounded so judgmental.

"No. Well, the other kids in Damon's Mountains would sneak out of their houses at night and go skinny dipping at Bear Trap Falls, but not me. I was a good girl."

"What the hell do you see in me then, Goody Goody? I break all the damn rules, and just so you know, I'm gonna try to turn you bad, too. Challenge considered and accepted and all that."

"I already am bad." She pulled up the hem of his T-shirt to show him she was wearing zero panties.

The smile fell from his face, and his expression went slack as he stared between her legs. "I just went dumb, so if you want any more intelligent conversation from me tonight, you're shit out of luck, woman. Spread your legs wider so I can play gynecologist."

"Ew!" She laughed and clamped her knees together. "Don't say weird stuff."

Barret pulled her off the counter and tossed her over his shoulder like he really was Barret the Barbarian, then strode out the front door. He lifted the bottom of her shirt and smacked her ass quick. She jerked at the sting. "Barret!"

"You're welcome."

Click.

"What was that noise?" she asked, trying her best to twist around.

"You are so sexy wearing my shirt," he rumbled distractedly.

They were almost out of the circle of porch light that lit up the clearing. "Seriously, what was that clicking noise? Did you take a picture?"

"No." *Click.* "I took two pictures. You have a perfect pink handprint on your ass cheek. It's hot as fuck."

She could hear him poking buttons on his phone, so she tried to turn around again. "You can't send those to anyone!"

"Why the hell would I send them to anyone? These are for my personal spank bank."

"Oh, my gosh," she muttered.

"I'm making you an album. I named it Not Boring Eden. Don't worry, I won't tell Jaxon."

Eden caught a glimpse of the album he was adding the two horrifically embarrassing butt pictures to. She wiggled down him to the ground, then snatched his phone. Okay, the butt pictures weren't as bad as she'd expected since Barret grinned huge in both, like he was proud to have his face that close to her left cheek. The pictures were actually really funny. But what caught her attention were the other three he'd added to the Not Boring Eden album. One was of her walking away from him in the grocery store, the first time they'd met face to face. It was a little blurry, but yep, that was definitely her. Barret was walking quietly beside her now, and she looked up at him questioningly.

"I liked you since then," he said low. He shrugged. "I take pictures of stuff that feels important so I don't forget. I made myself forget about a lot of the stuff from when I was a kid, and I got really good at deleting stuff in my head. Too good maybe?" He cleared his throat. "You pissed me off at the store, but I didn't want to forget you."

Eden stopped and looked at the next picture. It was her climbing the stairs up to Lynn's tree house with bags of groceries in her hands."

"You kept humming," he said. "Marney used to sing." Barret cleared his throat. "Songbird. That's what my dad called her."

"Barret," she whispered, "that's what my dad calls my mom. She sings with the Beck Brothers at this local bar sometimes. She's got a pretty voice, and he's always called her that."

The corner of his lip twitched up, then fell almost immediately. "Marney had a pretty voice, too." *Twitch.* "Fuck."

Barret was trying. He was talking about Marney without her pushing. He was trying to share with her as much as he could before his panic set in. Good cat.

Eden held out the phone for him to see the next picture she was looking at. It was a sideways shot of them walking through the woods earlier tonight on their way to meet the Red Havoc Crew for dinner. She was talking, her mouth open as she formed a word, a smile on her lips and in her eyes as she looked up at Barret. He had his arm around her, holding her hand across her chest, and only part of his torso showed up in the image.

"I snuck that one because you were letting me touch you and you weren't running away." He dipped his gaze to her sneakers and then back up to her eyes. He said softly, "And I didn't want to forget."

"Do you have the rock still?" she asked suddenly. She had to know. "Do you have the rock I gave you?"

Barret frowned. "Of course." Smoothly, he pulled it out of his pocket, showed her, then shoved it deep in his jeans again. "It's my favorite present. I'm keeping it for always so I can think of you. Even after you go, I'll keep it." *Twitch*. "I got something for you."

"You did?"

"Well, I made it. I don't have a lot of money for presents for you, Eden, but I can carve things. My dad taught me how when I was a kid." *Twitch*. He pulled something small from his other pocket, but kept his fist closed around it. "I wanted to give it to you right after we fucked, but it didn't seem right to take you rough and then give you something like this. It's just a stupid little something." He shook his head self-deprecatingly, then shook her hand formally, squeezing something small and lightweight between their palms. And then he lifted her knuckles to his lips and pressed a lingering kiss there, eyes locked on hers. When he pulled away, he said, "Even after you go, I hope you keep that and think of me." And then he offered her a sad smile, turned, and walked toward the sound of water lapping a shore in the distance.

Stunned, she looked down at her palm. He'd carved her a small feather, stained it, and polished it to shining. And then he'd attached it to a thin cord of leather the same shade of light gray in her eyes.

He'd given her a gift but didn't realize how big it was. This was as important as a claiming mark to falcons. He'd accepted her gift, kept it, and then given her one in return. She would never tell him because she didn't want to trap him, but he'd just bound them in ways she couldn't explain. Her heart had already latched onto him, but as she stood in the dark Red Havoc woods with his gift clutched in one hand and his phone with her pictures in the other, she had a moment. Something big changed inside of her heart.

She reached the E.

And now she—Eden of the Ashe Crew, daughter of Kellen and Skyler Brown, albino falcon shifter, goody two-shoes lonely bird—became something else.

She became Barret's.

NINE

Eden stepped onto the pebble beach that lined the pond and scanned the surrounding woods. Where was Barret?

A loud "whoop!" sounded. Eden hunched in startlement as Barret went sailing through the air on a rope swing. He did a back flip and landed in the water with a goofy grin at her.

She belted out a laugh and gave a quick glance around to make sure no one was in the woods. There was nothing but the sound of the rippling water, Barret's breath as he broke the surface, and little mouse sounds somewhere on the forest floor behind her.

"Be the owl, not the chicken," Barret dared her.

God, she wished he knew what she was already. She wished he could say, "Be the falcon," and his lips would still stretch in the carefree smile he wore now, but instinct told her if she Changed in front of him, he would never give her that smile again.

Barret swam to her quick like he was born a damn merman, cupped his hands, and slapped the water, drenching her.

She gasped at how cold the water was and high-kneed it a few paces back. "Dick!"

"Works fine," he deadpanned, standing in the water and looking down at the body part in question. "You tested it out, remember? Get in the water so I can molest you."

"It's cold!"

"Then warm it up with your hot bod, Mystery Girl."

"I feel like that name doesn't apply anymore. You've been inside of me."

"It was perfect too, all warm and slimy—"

"Barret! Don't say slimy!"

"Woman, that was a compliment. Get in before I drag you in. Let's fondle."

She snorted. "Stop."

His baiting smile grew bigger. "You touch my nips, I'll touch yours."

Eden shook her head and tried to contain her smile, but failed. "I'm gonna do a strip-tease."

"Good. Make it weird."

Giggling, she wiggled her butt, then jumped around and swiveled her hips in a circle. She slapped her ass and looked over her shoulder with her eyes crossed and her cheeks puffed out.

"Oh, yeah, that's the move. Keep that shit up, you'll get a double-fucking tonight." Barret's stomach was flexing with laughter.

Quickly, and as un-seductively as she could, she struggled out of the wet shirt and whipped it around her head, then threw it on the ground. It made a sopping *slap* against the rocks. Barret was clapping and whistling now. Eden loved this. She could be completely silly, and he accepted it.

Laughing her head off, she pranced toward the water's edge, spanking the air with one hand, the other fist out in front, her boobs bobbing.

Barret was wearing the biggest, best smile she'd ever seen.

"God, you're fun," he told her as she tiptoed into

the waves.

Around ankle deep though, she hesitated because it really was cold. He was headed her way to meet her, and she thought he would toss her in the waves, but he didn't. He stooped slightly and picked her up like she was a queen, all folded in his arms. He ran the scruff of his two-day beard against the top of her head like an affectionate cat as he walked slowly to deeper waters. She was so touched by his unexpected sweetness, she slipped her arms around his neck and kissed his chest, right over his pounding heartbeat. It thumped faster against her lips, and she smiled, nuzzled him like an affectionate cat right back.

"I like you," he murmured. "You make me want to not kill things."

She looked up into his bright green eyes and brushed her knuckles against the rough whiskers on his cheek. "I calm you?"

He dipped his chin once. "Nobody's ever done that before."

"Are you saying I'm special?"

"Aw, don't get cocky now, Mystery Girl. I'm certified crazy. You should be running from me, not lookin' at me all mushy."

"You don't seem crazy to me."

"Then your crazy must match mine." He was hip-deep in the water now. "Take a deep breath. I'll dunk you quick so you get used to it. Going slow won't make it hurt less. Going slow never made anything hurt less."

"I trust you," she murmured, because he should hear that from her. She didn't just mean about the water temperature. *I trust you with my life*. That's what she was really saying. She hoped he would read between the lines because she was too cowardly to say it out loud.

Barret searched her eyes for a few moments, then leaned in and kissed her, lips soft against hers, plucking at her until he finally slid his tongue into her mouth and tasted her. It was a sweet kiss—the kind boys gave to girls they really liked. The kind that wasn't asking for more. The kind of kiss that was fine with staying a kiss, not transitioning to touches and sighs, hair pulling, gripping hips, bowing backs, and clutching covers.

She got lost here in the moonlit waves, kissing the man who had turned out to be everything she needed. It should be terrifying how fast this was happening, but this is how it had happened for her parents too, and the entire Ashe Crew. It had happened like this for all the shifter couples she knew. She used to think it was some kind of bonding magic that she didn't possess, but maybe her falcon was just waiting for Barret. These moments with him were full of butterflies, shocked gasps, warmth pooling low in her belly and spreading to her heart.

He moaned deep in his throat, once, twice, three times, in a sexy countdown before he lowered them into the water. Lips pressed hard against hers, he sank into the waves with her. The cold was shocking, but her body was still buzzing from Barret's kiss, from his touch, from his hands holding her under while he pulled her close to him at the same time. And still she trusted him. There was no struggle from her. Instead, she held onto his shoulders as he guided them to deeper water.

A few seconds of lips on lips at the bottom of the pond, surrounded by rays of blue moonlight and cloudy water, and then Barret pushed off the bottom and broke the surface. Eden inhaled deeply against his mouth, cold and warm all at once, her body in shock, her falcon steady, eyes on her mate. Her mate?

Yep, nothing had ever felt more right than that word in this moment. His hand cupped her cheek gently, like he was palming rose petals. A gentle touch from a rough man, he was good at showing care. He thought he was a broken monster, but to Eden, he had been broken into the perfect shape to fit her.

Barret was chaos, high walls, and jokes that hid his real parts from the world.

He was a disaster.

A beautiful, perfect, awe-inspiring disaster.

"You're *my* disaster," she whispered against his lips.

Barret froze and eased out of the kiss. He canted his head like a curious animal, one corner of his mouth turned up in an unsure smile. "I like that."

"Well, I like you."

The smile fell, and a frown marred his face. "Sometimes I want that more than anything, and then sometimes I think you shouldn't."

"Why not?"

"Because I want you to survive me."

"You wouldn't hurt me. I know you wouldn't."

"Not on the outside, Eden. I mean on your insides." He laid her on her back and held her floating there in the waves, spinning her slowly in the pond. "I wish I could take a picture of this. Of you, just like this, laid bare in these waves, wearing nothing but the necklace I made you, all shadowed by the moon, goosebumps all over, nipples drawn up, water lapping at your skin. Water can't you have you, though. Not tonight. Tonight you're just for me. I've never had anyone just for me. Not since Dad and Marney."

Eden's gaze went automatically to the tattoo of the falcon on his shoulder, but he didn't wince away this time. Instead, he allowed her to drink the artwork in. With a touch as light as a paintbrush stroke, she felt the perfect lines etched in ink below the falcon.

"Were these marks to remember the people you lost?"

He shook his head slowly, and his eyes went hard as stone. She could see the wall he was building as plain as day.

She was desperate not to lose the magic of the moment so she whispered, "It's okay not to talk about it. I can be patient."

"Sometimes I want to sabotage everything," he

murmured, still spinning her. "Fuck." His head jerked to the right, and he squeezed his eyes tightly closed for an instant, like the movement had hurt. Something about his memories made his body fight.

Oh, he couldn't give her answers on his tattoo yet, but he'd just given her something else—something big.

"When I think about the past, sometimes I get desperate not to get lost in the memories, and I mess shit up. On purpose. And even sometimes when I'm not thinking about the bad stuff, I want to ruin stuff for myself. Sometimes I push the Red Havoc Crew to the brink. Sometimes I dare Ben to kick me out, just to see if they're really with me. To see if he still thinks I'm salvageable. Sometimes I want to test you. I *will* test you. And then like an asshole, I'll sit back and gauge your reaction and look for an excuse to make you run away from me. Favorite color is red. Biggest fear is getting close to people. Now you go. Tell me something no one else knows. Tell me something big."

"Okay." Eden dipped down into the water and stood on the rocky bottom, facing him. She locked her eyes on him when she said, "Ben doesn't let you chase

Red Havoc off because you belong with them. I won't let you chase me off because I belong with you."

Barret inhaled sharply. "Don't say that." He angled his face away but kept his intense gaze on hers. "Don't say stuff that'll rattle around in my head after you're gone. I got enough ghosts in there."

"And what if I don't go?"

Barret backed off a couple steps into shallower water and scrubbed his hand down his jaw. "You shouldn't give hope like that to a man like me. It's a tease for a life I'm not built to keep."

"I'm not teasing."

"What can I offer a girl like you, Eden? Huh?" He sounded angry. "What could you possibly gain from being with me? I own an auto shop that's barely making it. I make half of my income making moonshine. I'm so fucked up I'm barely even a man."

"Stop."

"I have no family. I won't be a good dad to your cubs, and you deserve cubs, Eden!"

"Stop!" He was backing away, step-by-step, but she wasn't having it. "You're doing it now. You're sabotaging, and it's not going to work. Not with me. Barret, I'm serious. Stop!" When she lurched forward and grabbed his forearm, he paused, frozen in the pond, water at the middle of his stomach. She hopped up and threw her arms around his shoulders, held on tightly and said against his ear, "What can I gain by being with you? I don't give a shit about material things, Barret. Never have. I would gain you. It's enough. You're enough. Don't push me away." And then she lost her damn mind and sank her teeth into his shoulder.

He jerked, but he didn't stop her. He stood there like a statue for a moment, then gripped the back of her hair roughly and pulled her closer. "Harder or it won't scar," he snarled out. It had to hurt.

She was biting him hard, blood pooling in her mouth, but he wanted it to count, so…she made it count.

And the second she released his torn flesh from her bite, he repeated the words he'd murmured earlier, "Going slow never made anything hurt less." And then he sank his teeth into her shoulder, so fast and so hard she was stunned into stillness.

Oh, it hurt. It burned like fire and felt like he was biting her down to her bones. One second, and he changed her whole life. One second, and he picked her, not like with the present that he didn't know the significance of. This was him claiming her back. One second of pain, and he released her skin and crushed her against him. His breath hitched, and his hand went tight in the back of her hair as he rocked them gently in the waves. Warmth trickled down her shoulder and pooled in the crevice between their skin. Moonlight, crimson, warm and cold, warm and cold...love, love, *I love him*. Why was she crying? Tears were pouring down her face that she couldn't stop. All she could do was clutch onto him harder to keep from falling into a million pieces. Her chest burned with something she didn't understand, something that drew her to him.

"Shhhh," he crooned, swaying back and forth like a boy at a high school dance.

She suddenly regretted how long it had taken them to find each other. Oh, their life wouldn't be easy. No shifter's was, but they were going to walk through it together. She'd never thought she would be lucky enough to get a claiming mark and a gift, but he'd given her both. Her parents had always told her that when she met her match, she would know quick. It's how it worked, but a big part of her hadn't believed them. She'd believed instead that there was no match—not for her, the lonely bird.

"Can't leave now," he said in a hoarse voice that said he was as emotional as her. "Can't leave me. I'm sorry."

"Bad Cat. No apologies for that. I'm gonna be so good at moonshining."

There was this moment of silence, and then he snorted. She peeled into giggles and gripped his short hair in the back, looked up at Mother Moon, and sighed. "Can't get me to run now."

Barret took them deeper into the water and eased back just enough for his lips to crash onto hers. His arm was tight around her back as he pulled her against him and slid into her. She moaned into his mouth because this was perfect. It was the perfect ending to what they'd just done. He wasn't rough this time, no. He was true to his word, taking care of her for their second time. His hips moved slowly, smoothly as he pushed into her, eased out, pushed in and eased out. The man knew how to hit her just right. He was already building a fire in her middle, building the pressure, building her body's devotion to him. Inside, her falcon was screeching in possessive victory. *Mine. He's all mine.* For better or worse. For the broken days that would come. The days where they would have to work through Barret's past. For the perfect days that would break up the dark until the bad days were no longer. She could see their future so brightly.

Barret grunted this sexy sound, and his body was shaking now with every thrust into her. He was close, and she loved this. Loved falling together as he tried to keep control of himself for her. Faster, faster, he was bucking into her now just as fast as she needed it. So close. Eden threw her head back and closed her eyes when his lips went to her throat. Every inch of her skin that touched his was tingling and warm. Nothing had ever been like this—so intense. Barret had been worth the wait.

His arms went tight around her as he came, pulsing streams of warmth into her. His throbbing shaft spurred her own orgasm on. "Barret," she cried, "deeper!"

And he did. He pushed so deep into her there was no end to him, no beginning to her. Bodies pulsing, they moved together, graceful like the waves around them. Slower and slower, drawing every aftershock out as they coveted each other's bodies. And when they were spent, they held each other, no words here in the dark, just content to be in each other's arms.

She didn't know how long they stayed like that, with no one to witness this huge moment but them and the moon, but Barret whispered something against her ear that made her heart wrap around him completely. "Eden, I think I love you."

Her eyes filled instantly and spilled over onto her cheeks. Barret had broken her apart and put her back together in a different shape tonight—a better shape. She could feel the growth, feel the changes within her. No more would she be stagnant and alone.

"Barret, I *know* I love you."

"I told you," a voice echoed across the pond.

Barret turned with a snarl, stepped in front of Eden protectively. But Eden knew that voice like the back of her hand. Lynn.

"I told you not to fall in love," Lynn said. Her red hair was mussed, and she was wearing jean shorts and a red tank top, no shoes. "I knew something bad was happening. I felt it in my bones. Take it back!"

"What?" Eden asked, padding across the pond bottom to stand beside Barret.

Tears streaked down Lynn's face, and her blazing gold eyes were wide and panicked. She snarled up her lip. "I'm saving you. I told you both not to fall in love. Take. It. Back."

Eden shook her head sadly. "Barret isn't Brody."

"It's not you I'm worried about, Eden!" she screeched. "I know! I know! I know about the Four Deadlies. Take it back so he can be okay. He's been nice to me. He's broken like me. You're going to ruin him."

Barret shook his head. "I don't understand. Fuck." *Twitch.* "Lynn, Eden isn't hurting me."

Lynn dragged in a long, ragged breath, and her next words were like little grenades. "Tell him what you are."

Oh no. Eden shook her head hard at her friend. "Lynn, don't."

"You don't understand! Neither of you do. Love destroys everything. I can't save the rest of the crew from it, but I can save you. Brody took everything! I gave him my heart and he squeezed it in his hand—" Lynn's voice broke and her shoulders sagged with a sob. "He squeezed it in his hand until I was nothing at all. I'm nothing, and I don't want to do this anymore. I want you to survive, and you can't if you fall in love. No one can. Love is poison. Tell Barret what you are, or I will. Do it now. Tell him!"

Barret arched his hard gaze down to Eden, and something in his fiery eyes said he was starting to put it together. His chest was heaving as he took two slow steps back and faced her. He was moving too slow and graceful now, like a predator on the hunt. "You aren't an owl, are you?"

"Barret," Eden whispered, pleading. "I can explain."

His eyebrows twitched up, and he looked dangerous, his face all shadowed by the blue moonlight. "I don't want explanations. Show me."

Inside, her falcon was rising up to the challenge. She wanted to show herself, but her animal didn't understand. It was too soon.

"Eden," he gritted out, his nostrils flaring with fury. "*Show me.*"

Her face crumpled as her body exploded with the Change. Pain. She'd had him. She'd had his heart for a blinding, beautiful second. Feathers, talons, the screech in her throat as she raked her claws onto his shoulder, right next to the claiming mark she'd given him because, damn it all, she wanted him to remember the moment they'd had…to remember he was hers and she was his.

Her feathers were wet and heavy, so she had to work to get airborne. She beat the air with her huge wings and turned as she hit the first good wind current because she wanted to see his face.

His expression broke her heart. His jaw was clenched in anger, his eyes blazing bright green. And then he did something awful. He bunched his muscles, and his panther blasted out of his skin. He went airborne too, leaping for her, reaching his powerful arms toward her, claws extended, murder on his face.

But he's ours. Poor falcon, so confused in the second before his claw brushed the flight feathers of her left wing. He'd missed, but he'd tried. Tried to hurt her, tried to bring her down into the water.

Barret really was broken.

His damage was too big, and because of the animal she was, she wouldn't be able to fix him. Eden realized this all in the moment when he tried to drag her beneath the waves with him.

Below her, he fell back down into the water with

a massive splash while she climbed the currents higher and higher in desperation to put space between them. The ache in her chest that he'd made when he'd bitten her magnified until it felt like she'd swallowed a hot poker. The farther she flew away from him, the more she felt like she was dying. Maybe that's what broken hearts felt like—dying. Maybe Lynn had been right. Maybe love did destroy everything.

Lynn was on the bank, screaming something about lions. "Kill the lions!" Kill the lions? She really was crazy. What lions?

Barret hit the shore running, sopping wet, water flying from his tail and feet as he bolted for the woods. And then there were two panthers running. Lynn was with him, but they weren't headed back to the Red Havoc cabins. Where the fuck were they going?

Eden coasted over them, but it wasn't until they neared the edge of Red Havoc territory that warning alarms blasted through her body. Barret and Lynn were hunting. Lions? Fuck!

She dove for Barret. *Stop, please!*

He turned at the last second as though he could

feel her coming for him and swatted out a paw, hissed as he skidded through the dead leaves. He turned for her. Crap!

She desperately pummeled her wings against the air to lift out of his reach, but Barret was too fast. He used the trunk of a tree to get higher into the air as she aimed her body for the sky. Too close, too close! He bolted out onto a branch and leapt for her. Eden screeched in fear as she jerked backward. He missed her by an inch and landed hard on the ground. With a furious look up at her, he trotted after Lynn past the territory line.

Eden needed help. Those two panthers wouldn't be pulled off a hunt, and Lynn was insane, encouraging him to go after lions. Lynn was starting a war and using Barret's fury to fuel it.

Eden lifted above the canopy and flew as fast as she could toward the Red Havoc cabins.

She needed help.

She needed the Red Havoc Crew to stop this war.

She needed them to save Barret.

TEN

Ben was standing in the middle of the clearing in front of the houses, eyes on the woods in the direction of Barret and Lynn. He was still as stone, a frown marring his features, his eyes glowing gold in the halo of porch light he stood on the edge of.

Oh, the alpha had bad feelings, and he should. This was really, really bad. A war with lions could get the entire crew killed. *Help, help, help!*

She dove, and at the last minute spread her wings to slow herself like a parachute. She was coming in too fast though, and had to lift at the last second to miss Ben. Her Change had already started, so she hit the ground so hard it knocked her breath from her lungs.

Eden climbed up onto her hands and knees, gasping for air with the desperation to get a few words out. Fuck, she didn't have time for this. She slammed her fists on the ground and forced air into herself. Behind her, Ben gave a shrill whistle. "Red Havoc!! Something's wrong!"

"Help," she forced out.

Ben knelt beside her. "Up. Get up and straighten out your diaphragm. Greyson! Jax! Anson!" He dragged her up on her feet as she gasped for air.

"Lynn. Barret. Lions."

"They went after the lions?" Ben barked out, panic tainting his voice as the Red Havoc crew poured from their cabins at a sprint.

"Barret got mad at me. Lynn encouraged him to fight." *Gasp.* "They're past the territory line."

"Shit," Greyson muttered. "What's our move, boss?"

Ben's order was immediate and decisive. "You and Anson Change. Try to catch him. Now!"

Greyson and Anson crumpled inward immediately and landed on all fours. Greyson recovered first from the forced Change and took off, Anson following seconds later. Ben jammed a finger at Annalise. "We need She-Devil tonight."

"But I can't control her!"

"Good! Don't fucking control her! We've got two panthers in lion territory. Let that demon out! Kaylee, we need your lioness, too. Jenny, stay here with the cubs."

"Oh, yeah, leave me to worry about my whole goddamn crew being killed off!" Jenny yelled.

"Woman you can tear me a new one when I get back. And I swear I'm coming back to you, Jenny. We all are." Ben's gaze lingered a moment longer on his mate, and then he dragged a gasping Eden toward a jacked-up silver Dodge Ram. "Jax, you drive."

Jaxon was shirtless, and his fiery green eyes looked like they belonged to the devil himself. He'd always been scary as a grizzly, but something had changed about his human side since he'd left Damon's Mountains. He had a mate and a crew to protect now. Eden was glad in her choice to get the crew's help. *God, don't let it be too late.*

They piled into the truck, and Jaxon spun out of the clearing before they even had the doors all the way shut.

"You're a falcon," Ben said in a harsh tone from

the passenger's seat where he was holding onto the oh-shit bar. The truck was flying through the woods, skidding on tight curves, back end throwing muddy rooster tails and barely missing trees. "You're a fucking falcon!" Ben said again.

"So?" Jaxon yelled, tossing his alpha a glare. "Back off her. She was always a falcon."

"You don't know the history, Gray Back."

"Don't you fuckin' call me a Gray Back right now, Ben. I'm going to war for you. I'm crew."

"Crew? No one fucking listens to me! I put down an order for Barret not to go after the lions. An order! He doesn't listen, you don't listen, your bear is ready to bleed everyone all the time, your mate rampages daily, Anson has told so many dick jokes I want to drown myself, and now we've got a fucking falcon starting wars with the Cold Mountain Pride. You were right, you little shit flake. We are the C-Team!"

"A," Jaxon yelled, "I'm not little, and two, shits don't flake. Or if yours do, you need to go to the poop-chute doctor ASAP—"

"Shut. Up. Jax," Ben gritted out.

"Careful, Ben," Annalise snarled from beside Eden. She smelled like fur, and her voice was low and gravelly.

"No Changing in here," Ben demanded. "Not that anyone actually listens to my orders."

Jax turned up the volume on the radio to a rap song at full blast, but Ben immediately turned it back down. "Do you know what the falcons did to Barret's people?" he asked, twisting in the seat to glare at Eden. "What they did to his family? Of course he was gonna go off the rails!"

"Yeah, I know, but I'm not like them! I was raised by good people!"

"Amen," Jax said.

"Stop it," Ben growled at the driver. "You're not helping."

This was taking too long, and the arguing was riling up her falcon. Eden had her breath back now, so she rolled down the window and started climbing out.

"What are you doing?" Kaylee cried, reaching across Annalise to clutch at Eden's legs.

"Let her go," Jaxon muttered.

"No! Shifter healing can only do so much!" Kaylee yelled, gripping her ankle and pulling her back inside.

"Let me go!" Eden said. "I'll Change before I hit

the ground. I have to help. I have to buy Barret time for you to get to him."

"Why?" Ben asked suddenly.

There was a moment of silence when Eden's eyes burned with tears at the thought of admitting her feelings, because she knew deep in her heart Barret couldn't feel the same way about her now. Not when he knew what she was. "Because I love him. He has to live or I won't live."

There was a loaded moment of silence, and then Ben said, "Let go of her leg, Kaylee. Eden, protect my cat. Protect Barret. Buy him time."

"I will. I promise." She hoped with all her heart she would be able to keep that promise. The car jerked hard, and she gripped the open window, gave Jax a quick glance. He looked back at her and nodded. "You've got the blood of a Crestfall warrior running through you, Eden, and the blood of Kellen. Let the War Bird out."

With a cry for the pain, to urge her falcon out of her, Eden pushed out of the window and let the animal have her. In an instant, she was airborne, beating her wings toward the top of the canopy so she could find her mate.

Frantically she searched the ground through the breaks in the thick trees. Movement caught her eye thirty seconds into her search, and there were Greyson and Anson, tearing through the woods below. Eden pushed her wings, flew faster than she ever had, searching the ground desperately. There were lights in the woods ahead, and when she got close enough, she could see five big cabins. It was some sort of fancy log cabin resort. The clearing in front of the homes was lit up with towering baseball stadium lights, making it so bright it looked like daytime. Below, there was a pile of violence—two panthers and four fully mature male lions. The war had begun. There was a scream of pain. Lynn? Fuck.

Barret was protecting her, spinning, keeping the pile of big cats off Lynn, but he looked bad off. His fur was wet and matted. Eden tucked her wings and dove straight for them.

Don't fall in love.

Fuck that. It was advice she couldn't listen to. Love wasn't something to be controlled. It was a storm to get wrapped up in, and all she could do was hang onto Barret and hope he kept her heart safe, like she would keep him safe. Love wasn't a faucet. There was no turning it off when it was convenient.

Jax's advice was better. *Let the War Bird out.*

With a screech to warn them of the hell that was coming for them, Eden stretched out her massive talons and dragged the lion off Barret's back. The brute was too heavy to lift, but Eden didn't let go until she'd cut him across the back with her razor talons. He roared in pain.

Run beast. I'm coming back for you.

She spun quick and dove again, sliced up the face of another lion with a black mane and scars all over his body. Over and over she dive-bombed them, barely missing claws to her body, twisting, spinning out of the way, using every bit of agility Mom had taught her in her training to protect herself from other falcons. Lynn was at the bottom of the pile, not moving anymore, and there was this moment when Eden latched onto a lion that was going after Lynn's neck that she came face-to-face with Barret. His eyes were glowing green, locked on hers, and his face was snarled up with fury and pain. Time slowed as her claws dug into the lion's neck, and for an instant she thought Barret would swat her from the air himself. He snarled his lips back at her and leapt, but he wasn't angled right. He slammed into her sideways, and then there was pain—so much pain as she rolled, end over end, tucking her wings to try and save them from being broken. It wasn't until she struggled up out of a long trench she'd made in the dirt that she realized what Barret had done. He'd put himself in front of a lion that had been going after her. He was in a brawl to the death with the monster cat. Spinning, growling, clawing, biting...defending her.

Barret wasn't lost to her. His panther was protecting her, just like he had before.

Her body hurt. She'd hit a rock, and red was staining her breast feathers. Red and white, red and white. Too much, but Barret needed her. She could hear the battle cries of Red Havoc—the roar of a grizzly, the screams of panthers, the bellow of a lioness. Eden could see them charging into the fray, but Barret was brawling injured. Such a deep well of protectiveness overtook her. He was hers to protect for always. Fuck the pain. She pushed up into the air and dove for the lion, pulled at his hind quarters to distract him with pain. He spun and almost slapped her down to earth, but she twitched out of his reach at the last instant.

Buy him time.

Barret was back on him, teeth sunk deep in the lion's shoulder.

The lion reached around and encircled Barret with his massive arms, claws raking her mate's ribs.

Buy him time.

Eden went for the eyes. It was dangerous. It was risky. She was too close to teeth and front claws, but this was a move of sheer desperation as the battle raged in the background.

There was a moment when time stopped completely. It was as if she had taken a picture in her mind and had time to study it. Her body was rigid, talons aimed at the lion's face, wings above her head, and Barret was in a deadly embrace with the lion. Beside her, Jaxon's massive grizzly was leaping through the air, murder in his shining eyes, and She-Devil with her spots was mid-air, claws out, both of them aimed for the same lion.

Eden couldn't stop her trajectory and she was about to be buried under a mountain of monsters.

Barret let off a terrifying scream and gave the lion his neck to reach out for her. All she could do was finish what she started because Barret was in danger of a kill bite. Damn the consequences, she had to do this. She could see the intention in that lion's eyes as he went for Barret's throat. He was in this to kill her mate.

Buy him time.

She latched onto the lion just as his teeth pierced Barret's neck, and he jerked back in shock. Time sped up again, and everything happened in an instant. Barret pulled her to his chest and ducked, covering her with his body just as a great weight hit him, knocking him sideways and throwing them across the grass. He grunted with the force, but didn't loosen his grip on her.

And then an eerie calm came over the clearing. Eden's body hurt so bad. Every inch of her felt cut and scraped and bruised and broken. She didn't want to look at herself, and even if she wanted to, Barret had her pinned and covered. So she dared her eyes open and watched the four lions fleeing into the woods, chased by the Red Havoc Crew. All but Greyson, who was human and standing over them, face canted, eyes gold, a worried set to his mouth as he stared down at Barret.

Barret opened his eyes slowly, and his pupils

constricted to pinpoints as he focused on her. He hissed long and low, exposing his long, curved canines.

"Barret," Greyson warned. "It's just Eden. She's good. She's yours." He was inching closer to her, which was terrifying because his careful posturing meant Greyson thought Barret might still hurt her.

Eden's heart pounded against her breastbone as she laid there in the grip of the man she loved, not knowing whether he would nuzzle her face or snap her neck. He did neither. He backed away suddenly, belly dragging the ground as he screamed an ear-piercing sound for Greyson as he slunk past him. He stood and glanced between her and Greyson, back and forth, looking utterly confused, tail twitching in irritation, his ears laid back, blood soaking his slick, black coat and streaming from his belly to the grass, painting the earth in crimson.

Barret snarled up one side of his mouth and licked red from his lips, then meandered toward the woods and didn't look back. He wasn't even limping, as if he felt no pain at all.

Greyson twisted his torso and looked down at her. "Shit, Eden, you got all tore up." A slow smile spread across his face. "Atta girl. I saw you. Your man is upright because you got to him fast enough. That's how you do the damn thing."

Eden heaved breath, still trying to catch it. She looked over at Lynn. Jaxon was back, human, kneeling over her. Lynn had Changed back too, and was lying on her side, facing Eden, staring at her with vacant eyes. Her arms were crossed over her chest, and she was shivering. Claw marks crisscrossed her body, but she didn't show any pain.

Ben and the others strode out of the tree line and gathered around them in a loose circle.

"Barret?" Ben asked.

"He'll live," Greyson murmured. "He's running again."

"I wanted it to end," Lynn whispered.

Ben inhaled sharply. "Wanted what to end?"

"Me. I didn't want to go alone, though. I made Barret come with me so I wouldn't be alone at the end. He's broken, too. He could've gone with me, and it would've been okay. Everything would've been okay."

Eden forced her Change as her heart broke at her friend's words.

She crawled to her, holding her stomach where she'd been cut in the battle. Tears dripping from her jaw, she gathered Lynn's head into her lap and cradled her close, rocking. "Don't say things like that, Lynn. Everything will be okay. You have to stay here with me and keep fighting, though." Eden swallowed a sob. "I need my friend here with me."

"Nobody needs me," Lynn whispered. She closed her eyes and squeezed out two tears, then turned and buried her face against Eden's leg. "I want it to end. Ben...make it end."

Ben looked instantly gutted. He shook his head over and over and linked his hands behind his hair, backed up a few steps like he'd been punched. "Lynn—"

"I'm serious," the frail woman whispered, shoulders shaking.

Jaxon squatted down right next to them and stared at Lynn with ghosts in his eyes.

"This war was her doing," Anson murmured, his arm around Kaylee. "She put us at risk trying to end it, and we have two cubs to protect in the crew."

"Anson, I know what's at stake," Ben gritted out. "One of those cubs is mine."

"There's no improvement," Anson continued.

"Stop!" Ben said, slashing his hand through the air. "I need a minute. I have to think."

"She's asking, man. She's asking for you to put her down. She's too far gone. She could've gotten us killed tonight, and you think the pride would stop with us? Fuck no. They would've gone straight to the cabins and—" Anson swallowed hard and shook his head at the direction of Red Havoc Woods. "I don't want her put down, but sometimes this has to happen. You know it and I know it." Anson jerked his chin toward Lynn. "She knows it."

"How about," Eden gritted out, "if anyone tries to put her down, I'll fucking murder you. I dare you to try." She inhaled and yelled, "I dare you!"

Ben was pacing back to them, his eyes full of heartache. "Eden, I've waited for her to get better, but her broken mate bond hurts her. And then her giving away her cub? She has no anchor. Do you understand what I'm saying? For a minute, I hoped it would be you, but it's not. You came to help her, and she still tried to end it."

Eden gathered Lynn's frail body closer. "Jaxon." She gave him a pissed off glare and dared him to deny her.

Jaxon locked eyes with her and looked like he'd aged ten years in a few minutes.

"Jaxon!" Eden said again. "She's from home. She was raised right outside of Damon's Mountains. She's one of us."

"She's part of this crew and under an alpha who can make these decisions."

"Jax, please," she begged. "Lynn's my best friend. She needs more time."

His eyes rimmed with moisture, and he wiped his cheek on his shoulder fast. And then he stood and put himself between Ben and Lynn. "I'm asking your permission to take her back to the Gray Backs. I'll have my brother pick her up. Give Creed a chance to rehab her. Last chance for her. If he can't do it, I won't stand in the way of her being put down." He turned and looked down at Eden. "Neither will Eden."

"Do you know what you're asking of me?" Ben yelled, hooking his hands on his hips. "Do you? The last troubled shifter I let go was Brody, and he went out in the world and did awful things. Innocent blood is on my hands because I didn't put him down when I should've."

Lynn curled in on herself and went quiet with her crying. Her eyes went vacant again as she stared off into the woods.

"Please," Eden begged.

"Vote on it," Jaxon said low.

Ben snarled up his lip and did an immediate thumbs down. Anson did the same, and so did Greyson. They looked heartbroken about it, but they were voting to end her. Kaylee gave her mate an apologetic look, then put her thumb up. So did Jaxon and Annalise. Lynn lifted her shaking hand in the air and did a thumbs down.

Greyson murmured, "It's a draw. We can wait to see what Jenny and Barret vote for."

Ben snarled and paced toward the woods and then back again. "No, we don't have to. I know how they will both vote. Jax, make the call to Jathan. He needs her in hand by next week. Creed has one month to fix Lynn, and then I'm granting her wish. I have to. It's my job. I'm alpha, and it's the worst part about this, but someone has to make the hard decisions." He spat in the mud, eyes blazing and face twisted in a feral expression. And then the alpha walked away without looking back.

The others followed one at a time until it was just Eden, Jax, and Lynn left.

"Thank you," Eden murmured.

Jax stood and threw a stick he'd picked up into the woods. "She ain't saved yet, Eden. You bought your man time tonight. That's all you did for Lynn. You bought her time. You can't save people who don't want to be saved." He gave her one last fiery look, then strode off behind the rest of his crew.

And then it was just Lynn, a broken panther, and Eden, a broken-hearted falcon determined to fix the ones she loved, whether they wanted fixing or not.

ELEVEN

Barret yanked the wrench over and over, desperate to get the bolt to move on the old beater truck, but all he was doing was stripping it. He only came to the shop at nights when he was running away from the memories. When he was desperate to do mindless work on a car.

Tonight had gone so wrong. His entire world had been stripped to nothing...again. He'd bonded. Him. Broken Barret the Barbarian. Murder Kitty. He'd found his match against all odds. He'd found someone who accepted his darkness, but how could he and Eden get past this?

He'd lost her. How could he keep her now? Her people had killed his people, and he'd been hunting.

He'd been taking revenge on the falcons who had stolen everything away. The blood of her people was on his hands too. Everything had gotten so messed up. Fuck the Fates who decided to give him a falcon. It was a tease. It was a good life dangled in front of an unsalvageable man, and then ripped away.

Sleep my boy
For I am near…

The sound of wings beating the air overpowered his senses, and he covered his ears. He gripped the wrench as hard as he could as he closed his eyes and gritted his teeth. "Leave me alone!"

Fucking ghosts, fucking ghosts…he could feel the spray of warmth across his face.

Hide in here, little cat. If ever there comes a day when you need to run away, hide in here, and I'll be with you.

"Liar!" Barret covered his face and screamed as long and as loud as he could just to rid himself of Marney's voice.

It wasn't working. She was singing again, softly, like she wanted attention. He used to sit on the rug by the fireplace and listen to her play guitar and sing songs she'd made up. She was so good. Good voice. *Twitch*. Fuck. *Twitch*. Fuck!

He slid out from under the truck on the creeper, and stood in a rush, desperate to get the memories to stop flooding him. His chest cavity felt like it was full of fire, and panic seized him. "I'm dying!" He chucked the wrench and knocked over a tool box. Metal clanged deafeningly across the floor. Barret gripped his hair and squatted down.

Dying and alone. It was as if he was in the cave, hiding from the falcons all over again.

"Shh," said a voice. A real one. And then a hand was on his back. He froze and inhaled, scenting the air. Greyson.

With a sigh of anguish, Barret slumped over against his leg. "She's a falcon, Grey."

Greyson pulled him tighter against his leg and murmured, "She ain't like them. She was raised outside of the Crestfalls."

"And when they come for her? Fuck." *Twitch*. "When they come to kill her and I can't save her?"

There was another hand. Ben. Gripping his shoulder.

Another. Jaxon, hand on Barret's head.

Another. Kaylee, sitting beside him.

Another. Annalise, kneeling behind him, palm on his spine.

Another. Jenny. Hand gripping the back of his hair.

Warmth was blanketing him, stretching from their touch, but it wasn't enough.

Hide in here, and you'll be safe. Don't come out until the sky is clear, okay little cat?

"Tell us," Eden said from the doorway. "Let us hold the memories with you. You're strong, Barret, the strongest man I've ever known, but this is too much for one man to carry alone."

"You know. You know what happened. You lied to me. You knew what happened to the Four Deadlies, and you hid your animal from me."

Eden approached slowly, and then she did something that shocked him to his core. Despite the long, rattling rumble of his snarl scratching up his throat, she straddled his lap and hugged him tight, as if she had no survival instincts at all.

"I was so afraid I would lose you because I did know what happened to your crew. None of the details, just the end result. I was afraid you would see my animal and hate me."

He swallowed hard and hugged her against his chest, clutching her shirt. "When I tell you, you will be the one who leaves. You'll be the one who hates me."

She eased back and searched his face. "I don't understand."

Barret licked his lips and wished to God he didn't have to do this. He angled the tattoo toward her and pointed to the marks. "Those aren't losses, Eden. They're kills."

She looked at the marks, all ten of them, then back to him and then to the marks, utter confusion in her pretty blue-gray eyes.

"I'm halfway through the Welkin Raider's council."

Realization washed across her face like a tidal wave. "You were the one who killed the Crestfall council members?"

"I waited until I was a man and I knew what it was to take a life before I sought vengeance for the Four Deadlies. If I didn't do it, who would? I was the only one left."

You're too angry, Barret. Be calm, little cat. You're safe.

"Fuck," he gritted out, shaking his head to rattle the ghost free. "Your feathers are white like your hair. I thought you were a snowy owl. What is your lineage? I can't tell from your feather markings. You barely have any." *Please let her not be a Crestfall.*

Eden's face crumpled, and he hated himself for hurting her. "My lineage is on the Crestfall side. You killed my grandfather. He was on the council."

Barret's heart dropped down to the floor. Jax muttered a curse, paced away and then back before resting his hand on Barret's head again.

"I didn't know. I didn't know. I didn't know I would choose a falcon," Barret forced out. "I didn't mean to hurt you. I made it look like part of the war."

Eden's shoulders were shaking, and she buried her face against his chest. "I never met him. I haven't met any falcons other than my mom."

"But Eden, how can we be together now? Even if you haven't met them, I killed part of your family—"

"Stop. Barret, stop! The falcons are bad. My parents and Damon Daye went to great lengths to keep me and my coloring a secret from them. My grandfather would've sent warriors into our mountains to retrieve me if he knew there was a white falcon there. My own grandfather would've put me in their breeding program, just like he did to my mom. You didn't hurt me by killing him, Barret. You made me safer without realizing it." She gripped the back of his hair, forcing him to look at her, and now her entire body was trembling against him as she locked her churning silver gaze on his. "Tell me about Marney." Would she let him touch her with his hands? He had to try. He needed his palms against her skin. Touch meant forgiveness, right?

He pulled her against his chest, and she allowed it but didn't wrap her arms around him. She just sat in his lap, arms tucked between them. His heart felt like it was being shredded by the thought of admitting what he'd done, but she should know the reasons he hunted the falcon councils.

"My dad had a broken mate bond. He was headed where Lynn is, except he had an anchor. He had me, but I wasn't enough. I wasn't nearly enough to keep him okay. Two years into his spiral, two years into me not being touched or talked to or cared for...two years of feeding myself and getting myself to school and feeling completely alone in that house with him, Marney came, and she changed everything. My dad was like this flower. He opened back up, started living again. She didn't let him give up. She fixed the broken parts of him, but she wasn't a panther. The Four Deadlies' alpha balked at her being there because of the falcon wars, but he was an understanding alph—"

I love you, little cat. You're the son of my heart.

"Fuck." *Twitch.* "I don't want to do this. I don't want to do this."

"Get it done, Barret. Please just get it out before it poisons you," Eden pleaded. Her voice was so small he held her tighter, as if to hold her breaking pieces together, but really he was trying to keep himself together.

"The alpha let her stay, and we were happy. So happy. She was a good step-mom, a good mate for my dad. She brought us both back to life and made me feel safe and not alone." His voice broke, so he cleared his throat before he continued. "We were quiet with her shifter, and she only Changed at night. We wanted to keep her off the radar of the falcons forever, but we failed. We knew from the beginning that either the Crestfalls would come to put her back in the breeding program she'd escaped from or the Welkin Raiders would come to kill her. No one leaves the falcons. They don't let their people escape, or the females would wise up and all flock away from them. War happened on a Thursday. The Raiders had found her, and they were there to kill her. The Four Deadlies tried to protect her, and protect me." His voice went thick. "It was stormy, Marney's favorite weather. It was early in the morning. The panthers in my crew were screaming outside. Fuck." He could see it so clearly, the memories he'd worked so hard to tuck away in the darkest corners of his mind. It was like a movie playing right in his head. "I'm dying." God, he sounded pathetic.

"No, no, no, you're still here. With me," Eden said, wrapping her arms around his torso.

Barret rubbed his face against hers on one side, then the other, then rested his chin on her shoulder and stared at the night sky out the open garage door. "The panthers were screaming. Dad told me and Marney to stay in the house and lock the door. Marney was crying and saying it was all her fault. She was looking out the window with this look on her face as she watched the war... It was like she was dying inside. I could tell when my dad got killed—from her eyes, from the sound in her throat. She turned to me, and her eyes were empty. She told me to hide in the place she'd made for me in case the falcons ever came. 'Run, little cat. Hide, little cat. I'll come for you if I can. You have to run now so I can help the crew.' But I was ten and felt brave. I didn't want to leave Marney, so I followed when she went out the front door. I remember she walked with her arms out at her sides, palms up, her shoulders shaking, and her voice was broken when she screamed, 'You win! You ruined my life after all. You took everything good from this world just to hurt me.' And then she Changed and, God, she was fearless." He dragged in a hitching breath and squeezed his eyes closed. "She took the war to the air, drew the falcons up, up, out of my reach. When I was a cub, it felt like there were a hundred of them, but now looking back, there were probably just thirty in the sky. There were another twenty or so on the ground with the bodies of my crew. With the body of my dad. I was screaming for Marney to come back because I couldn't reach her. She was all I had left and I couldn't help her. There was a swarm of falcons on her, and something warm sprayed across my cheek as I was screaming her name over and over, "Marney! Marney! Mom!" I wiped off the raindrops, but it wasn't water on my fingertips. It was blood. Her blood. And then I watched her fall. And when she hit the ground and didn't move, I ran like she'd told me to do, and I hid in this little cave for three days, starving, thirsty, alone, replaying that awful day over and over in my head until I wasn't okay anymore and I knew I never would be again. On the third day, a man found me. A wild-looking man with bright green eyes who talked strangely. He said his name was Beaston, and he picked me up, hugged me for a long time, and then put me in his truck and bought me three hamburgers from this place in town. And then he drove me four hours to an old mountain man, a grizzly shifter who wasn't okay in society. And that old grizzly raised me. But he could never fix me."

Eden was crying so hard her body was shaking with her silent sobs, and from the sniffling around him, the others were emotional, too.

"So, there it is. There's the damage. Someday Ben

will put me down like he'll have to do for Lynn."

"Never," Eden said, easing back, stubbornness in her eyes. "I won't let you stay broken, Barret. I won't." Her cheeks and nose were red, and her eyes were full of tears. She looked hurt and fierce all at once.

"You should go back to Damon's Mountains. You'll be safe there."

"I'm safe with you."

"Except I can't save anyone, Eden. I only kill, not save."

"Says the man who defended my body against your crew. Says the man who was defending Lynn's body from an entire pride of lions tonight. Says the man who protected me during that same fight. You're breathing still because of me." Eden cupped his cheeks gently. "And I'm breathing because of you."

"Eden, the falcons will come for you. They always come. They'll draw you into their breeding program, or they'll kill you. You feel like mine, and I don't hurt so bad around you. You feel like my future. Like my steady. Like my heart. I bit you for a reason. Claimed you for a reason. You feel like everything that's good. Like everything that could make me better someday. You can save me, but I'm one man against two armies, and I've seen my limits before. What if I can't keep you safe?"

"Then I'll help," Annalise murmured from behind him.

"Me, too," Kaylee said.

Jenny nodded and squeezed his arm. "Me, too."

"Yep," Greyson said.

Jaxon threw up two fingers. "Same. That's what crews do. We've got your back, man, always. We've got your mate's back, too." Jaxon winked. "Even if she's boring and annoying."

Eden laughed thickly.

"Why not?" Anson said. "War with the lions, 'cause you know that shit ain't over, and now stirring a war with the falcons. Yep, I'm up for bad decisions. I'll help."

Ben was the last to speak. He looked exhausted and let off a long sigh. "All I wanted was to have a few bachelor panthers out in the woods, make moonshine, maybe get a beer together every once in a while. And what did y'all do?" He shook his head huffed out a soft breath. "You went and made us into a family." His mouth twitched into a slight smile. "At least life with you idiots is never dull. I'll help protect your mate, Barret, because I've seen good changes in you since she came into your life. In such a short time, she got you to open up and own the shit that happened. She'll save me from ever having to put you down. I know she will. You gotta War Bird fighting for you now. Eden?"

"Yes?" she asked softly, intertwining her fingers with Barret's and holding his hands so tightly. Hope pooled in her pretty eyes. God, he loved her.

Ben sighed and shook his head at Barret, but he was still wearing that tiny smile. He blinked slowly and gripped Eden's shoulder, locked his gaze on hers. "Welcome to the Red Havoc Crew."

TWELVE

Eden watched the Tahoe with the rental plates pull away. Jathan Barns, Jaxon's identical twin, glanced up at her one last time in the rearview mirror. His eyes were dark and somber, as though he knew what a long shot this was.

From the passenger's seat beside Jathan, Lynn never looked back. She'd refused to say goodbye to Eden or any of the crew. She was angry, but she was still here, and that was more important to Eden.

She stood in the middle of the dirt road, in the shadow of Lynn's tree house, watching her friend disappear and hoping Creed, alpha of the Gray Backs, could save her.

"She's angry," Barret said, slipping his arms

around her from behind.

"Angry with me."

There was a smile in his voice when he said, "Anger's good. Anger fuels a fight, and I haven't seen any fight in Lynn in a long time. You did good buying her time. Anyone else would've quit, but you don't quit on people. It's one of the things I love about you."

With a smile, she turned in his arms and looked up at him. The saturated midday sunlight was so bright she had to squint, and for a moment it looked like Barret wore a halo. She laughed. Her man wasn't a halo type of man. He said "fuck" too much.

With a happy sigh, she asked, "Wanna know something I love about you?"

"Barf!" Anson said from above where the crew was cleaning out Lynn's tree house. "Gross, yak, stop. We can all hear you being disgusting."

"It's not disgusting, it's romantic," Kaylee said primly from where she was sweeping leaves off the decking above.

Eden laughed and slipped her arms over Barret's shoulders. "I love that you let your walls down last week. And I love that you've let me in so much since then."

"You feel safe."

She couldn't help her beaming smile. "We're a safe place for each other."

Her Bad Cat glanced at the sky and back to her. He did that a lot now, and she didn't know if it would ever really go away—that feeling he could lose her like he'd lost Marney and his crew. But she did know one thing…

She was going to stay steady for him, always, so he could have a fighting chance at staying happy. Because his happiness fueled hers. She'd never smiled so much over the course of her entire life as she had in this past week. Funny mate, caring mate, complicated mate, protective mate. There were a hundred layers to Barret, and she loved every one. The more of his soul he exposed through those cracking walls, the deeper she bonded to him.

"You know when I gave you that rock and said it was a reminder that you could be good?"

His lips curved up into a sexy, crooked smile. "Yeah."

"I chose you then. Falcons give each other presents. I didn't tell you when I gave it to you, but I hoped you would keep it so I could pretend you were mine."

Barret leaned down and sipped her lips. When he eased away and she opened her eyes, he had the stone she'd given him on his palm. "I pretend, too," he murmured low. "I pretend this is your heart, and you gave it to me for safekeeping. Lynn said Brody took her heart and squeezed it and that love is poison. That's not us, Eden. I'll protect your heart always. I'll never lose it." He shoved the stone deep into his pocket again and then fingered her carved feather necklace that hung from her neck and rested just between her breasts. "When I gave you this, I chose you, too. I just didn't know how to tell you that without you running away."

"I'm not going anywhere," she promised. "I've had more happiness here, with you, with Red Havoc…" She shrugged and looked around. "I've found more happiness in these mountains than I've known my whole life. You make this place so special."

"No," he whispered, dragging his fingertip lightly down her cheek. "You're the special one. You feel like you're putting my insides back together."

"I'm like soul glue," she teased with a laugh.

"Sexy soul glue. We're gonna do bad things in

Lynn's tree house."

"Uuuh, that ain't Lynn's tree house," Jaxon said in an odd tone from where he stood by the railing at the bottom of the stairs.

Barret turned to him with a deep frown. "What do you mean?"

"Has anyone ever noticed this carving in the railing?"

"Yeah," Barret muttered. "1010 and a B."

Jaxon smiled at Eden, and then it hit her. "Beaston built this?" she asked, her voice pitched high.

"Beaston?" Barret asked, his eyebrows lowered in confusion. "The man who pulled me from the cave? The seer in the Gray Backs?"

Eden nodded in shock. "He must've known Red Havoc would settle here and built this tree house as a sanctuary." She approached the railing and, sure enough, Jax was right. The carving was clear as day. She'd passed it fifty times and never noticed it. Wow. The tree house was old. How long ago had Beaston traveled here and built this, knowing this crew would need it someday? Perhaps knowing Lynn would need it.

"I'm beginning to think things happen at certain

times for certain reasons," she said to Barret, slipping her hand into his.

"Me, too. Like when you came into my auto shop that first night, and then you *came* in my auto shop that first night." His smile turned devilish, and she laughed.

"No, I mean, the timing of Lynn calling me here, meeting you, claiming marks, working through the hard stuff, and going to war together and building our bond. And this tree house, built by a man who has touched both of our lives at different times. I found Red Havoc because everything fell into place just right. I found a crew where I'm not lonely because I met you." She swallowed hard. "I found a chosen family because of you. Thanks for letting me in."

Barret cupped the back of her head and pulled her forward until his lips pressed against her forehead. "Thanks for asking to come in. Thanks for not running when you saw my shadows. And also thanks for giving me blow jobs and helping me with moonshine deliveries."

She laughed and shoved his arm. "Why can't you just be serious and let us have a romantic moment?"

"Because they're gross," Anson called, staring

down at them over the railing above. "I keep saying that, but no one listens."

"Fuck you, man," Barret said. "You and Kaylee suck face all the time, and we all have to watch it and hear it, and *that's* gross."

"Who bought Lynn seven boxes of frozen burritos?" Annalise asked, her legs dangling from where she sat on the ledge of the deck above. She was holding one of the burritos in question in her hand.

"Me!" Barret said. "Don't judge me, *She-Devil*. I love burritos, so why don't you bite me?"

"I bite you like every day." Annalise gave him a beaming, unapologetic smile. "You're all gristle. It's why I spit you back out." She took a bite of the burrito and arched her eyebrows at him like she'd won.

"I hate all of you," Barret muttered. "Except Eden. She's cool."

Eden snorted and wrapped her arms around his taut waist. "You like me."

"No," he said, turning toward her and hooking a finger under her chin so she had to look up at him. "I L-O-V-E you."

Eden smiled so big her face hurt. That's how she thought of their story, too. Barret had reached the E, just like she had.

He kissed her once more, then swatted her ass and jogged up the first couple of stairs. On the third, he paused and turned to her. "You gonna stay with me?"

There was a bigger question in that than just her following him up into the tree house. With a sappy grin, she said, "Always."

His answering smile nearly stole her breath away. "Good." And then he turned and made his way up the stairs toward his crew. No...*their* crew. She was a part of this crazy C-Team of misfit shifters now, too.

What a dangerous, chaotic life she'd found, but what a beautiful one it was, too.

She climbed the stairs to join her mate and her people, and when she reached the deck, Barret was waiting for her with his arm outstretched so she could fit right against his ribs, that sly smile on his face that she loved so much. Jaxon and Anson were arguing. Ben looked annoyed. Greyson was quiet. Jenny, Annalise, and Kaylee were giggling, and below, the cubs were playing tag on the forest floor. Above, the sky was stormy, but peaceful, and the clouds were Barret's old favorite color, gray. It was as if

Marney was smiling down on them.

Eden didn't know what the future held for them, but in this moment, everything was perfect.

She wasn't the lonely bird anymore. She wasn't boring or on the outside.

Now she was Eden—War Bird, proud mate of the Bad Cat, fixer of the broken ones, and loyal member of the Red Havoc Crew.

Now…she was happy.

Want more of these characters?

Red Havoc Bad Cat is the third book in the Red Havoc Panthers series.

For more of these characters, check out these other books from T. S. Joyce.

Red Havoc Rogue
(Red Havoc Panthers, Book 1)

Red Havoc Rebel
(Red Havoc Panthers, Book 2)

This is a spinoff series set in the Damon's Mountains universe. Start with Lumberjack Werebear to enjoy the very beginning of this adventure.

About the Author

T.S. Joyce is devoted to bringing hot shifter romances to readers. Hungry alpha males are her calling card, and the wilder the men, the more she'll make them pour their hearts out. She werebear swears there'll be no swooning heroines in her books. It takes tough-as-nails women to handle her shifters.

She lives in a tiny town, outside of a tiny city, and devotes her life to writing big stories. Foodie, wolf whisperer, ninja, thief of tiny bottles of awesome smelling hotel shampoo, nap connoisseur, movie fanatic, and zombie slayer, and most of this bio is true.

Bear Shifters? Check

Smoldering Alpha Hotness? Double Check

Sexy Scenes? Fasten up your girdles, ladies and gents, it's gonna to be a wild ride.

> For more information on T. S. Joyce's work,
> visit her website at
> www.tsjoyce.com